DANGER AT THE END OF THE TRAIL

For the next ten minutes the only sound Stevie heard from ahead was the rushing river, growing louder with every step they took.

But then she heard something else.

"Help!"

Stevie froze. "Did you hear that?" she called over her shoulder.

"I heard it." Phil's voice was grim.

"Help!" The voice came again, faint but unmistakable.

"That's A.J.," Stevie said, urging her horse forward a little faster. "He's in trouble."

Phil didn't reply, but Stevie could hear Teddy's hoofbeats coming faster, too. They rode in silence for another minute or two before suddenly emerging from the dim shelter of the trees onto a rocky plateau running down a hundred yards to a wide, boulder-studded section of the river.

Stevie stared in horror. A.J. and Crystal had plunged into the rushing, foam-flecked water.

**Don't miss any of the excitement
at PINE HOLLOW,
where friends come first:**

And coming in April 2000:

PINE HOLLOW™

GROUND TRAINING

BY BONNIE BRYANT

BANTAM BOOKS
NEW YORK • TORONTO • LONDON • SYDNEY • AUCKLAND

Special thanks to Sir "B" Farms and Laura and Vinny Marino

RL 5.0, AGES 12 AND UP

GROUND TRAINING
A Bantam Book / February 2000

"Pine Hollow" is a trademark of Bonnie Bryant Hiller.

ISBN 0-553-49300-0

Visit us on the Web! www.randomhouse.com/teens

**Educators and librarians, for a variety of teaching tools, visit us at
www.randomhouse.com/teachers**

Published simultaneously in the United States and Canada.

Bantam Books is an imprint of Random House Children's Books, a
division of Random House, Inc. BANTAM BOOKS and the rooster
colophon are registered trademarks of Random House, Inc. Bantam
Books, 1540 Broadway, New York, New York 10036.

PRINTED IN THE UNITED STATES OF AMERICA

OPM   10 9 8 7 6 5 4 3 2 1

My special thanks to Catherine Hapka for her help in the writing of this book.

ONE

I don't think I can do this. Do I really have to? There must be another way, Carole Hanson thought as she pushed open one of the big double wooden doors of Pine Hollow Stables. She automatically took a deep breath, inhaling the warm, familiar hay-scented air. *How am I ever going to survive this day?*

She figured she must have asked herself the same question at least a thousand times since the previous afternoon, hearing it echo inside her head over and over again like an important plot point in a bad made-for-TV movie. But asking the question didn't bring her any closer to an answer. It didn't make it any easier to do what she had to do.

Today was the day I was going to mix the feed for the week, as usual, she thought as she walked slowly across the wide stable entryway. *And update the boarder files. And start planning the Thanksgiving holiday exercise schedule. And maybe get in a nice long training session with Firefly. But instead—*

"Carole!" Stevie's familiar voice broke into her thoughts.

Carole turned and saw her best friends, Stevie Lake and Lisa Atwood, coming toward her from one of the stable aisles. Noting Lisa's melancholy expression, Carole suddenly felt a new pang, one that had nothing to do with her own problems. The day before, while Carole and Stevie and most of the other Pine Hollow regulars were at a horse show, one of Pine Hollow's most beloved residents—a beautiful Thoroughbred mare named Prancer—had died. Prancer had been Lisa's favorite mount for years, and while everyone at the stable was shocked and saddened by the sudden loss, Carole knew the tragedy was hitting Lisa harder than anyone else.

"Hi," Carole said, forgetting about everything but Lisa's grief as she waited for her friends to reach her. She kept her gaze trained on Lisa's face. "How are you?"

Lisa did her best to smile. "I've been better," she said, pushing her silky blond hair behind one ear. She glanced around the entryway, which was deserted except for the three girls. "It's weird. Being here, I mean. It makes me think that it can't possibly be true—she can't really be gone." She paused, swallowed hard, and blinked a few times. "But at the same time, I guess I'm starting to realize that she is. It's not a bad dream, and I'm not going to wake up and find out she's still alive."

Stevie put an arm around Lisa's shoulders and squeezed briefly. "I know. I think it's just starting to hit home for all of us. But we'll all get through this together. Remember, you have a lot of friends who want to help. You don't have to do this alone."

As she spoke, Stevie forced herself to keep a calm, reassuring expression on her face, even though she wanted to bawl like a baby whenever she thought about Prancer. She was doing her best to stay as upbeat and supportive as possible. She couldn't remember a time when her two best friends had needed her more, and she wanted to do everything in her power to help them through their problems. The only trouble with that plan was that there didn't seem to be much that she could do, aside from letting them know that she cared.

It's not easy staying strong for them, she thought sadly. *Not when I can't seem to stop thinking about how Prancer looked yesterday—so helpless, like every breath was a struggle—and then remembering how* alive *she looked that day so many years ago when we saw her race . . . or all the shows when she competed her heart out for Lisa . . . or just*

3

the everyday sort of stuff, like how she used to nip at Belle on the trail when she got too close, or how she'd switch her tail back and forth whenever you scratched her in the right spot on her neck. . . .

Stevie felt herself getting teary as she thought about all the great years they'd spent with Prancer, all the ways she'd been such an important part of their lives. She swiped at her eyes, making sure that Lisa and Carole didn't see.

And somehow, she thought, glancing at Lisa again, *it makes it even harder to know that Lisa thought Prancer was finally going to be all hers, and now she's gone for good.*

It didn't seem fair somehow. Just recently, Lisa's father had arranged to buy Prancer from Max Regnery, the owner of Pine Hollow. He'd been planning to surprise Lisa with the mare as a very special gift for her high-school graduation in the spring. But Lisa had found out the secret early, and Stevie knew she'd been thrilled at the idea of owning the gentle mare she loved so much. Of finally having Prancer all to herself. And now Prancer was gone. No, it really didn't seem fair at all.

"Stevie's right." Carole spoke up, putting a hand on Lisa's arm. "Just let us know if there's anything we can do."

Carole's comment snapped Stevie's mind out of the past and back to Carole's situation. She was still trying to figure out how to feel about that. *I never would have guessed she was capable of cheating on a test,* she thought, glancing at Carole out of the corner of her eye.

It was a strange thought. Carole was one of Stevie's best friends, and she knew her about as well as she knew anyone. How could something like this happen without her even being aware of it?

I guess everyone makes mistakes, she thought. *It's just that I never thought Carole would make this particular kind of mistake. Flunking a test because she got too caught up with horses—that I'd have no trouble believing. But cheating on a test? It's no wonder her dad freaked out. It's not something any of us would have expected from her in a quadrillion years.*

"So what did the colonel say after you got home yesterday?" she asked Carole tentatively. "I hope he didn't pull the same thing as my parents did—you know, keeping me in suspense about how long I'm grounded."

Carole kicked at a stray clod of dirt on the stable floor. "No," she said. "That's not Dad's way. He wants me to know exactly how long I'm going to be stuck in the brig."

Stevie nodded. Carole's father, Colonel Hanson, had served in the Marine Corps for many years before his recent retirement. He somehow managed to be easygoing and extremely precise at the same time. "So what's the damage?"

"New Year's," Carole said softly.

Stevie winced. It was no worse than she'd been expecting, but still, it was practically impossible to believe. Carole had lived and breathed horses for as long as Stevie had known her. Even back in their junior-high days, when Stevie, Carole, and Lisa had formed a group called The Saddle Club so that they'd have an excuse to talk about horses as much as possible, Carole had stood out as the horse-craziest member of the trio. It was almost unthinkable that Carole would have to spend the next month and a half away from the stable, riding, her job—everything she cared about most.

Suddenly noticing that Lisa was staring off blankly into space, Stevie cleared her throat, searching for a way to distract her. It had been Stevie's idea to drag Lisa to Pine Hollow that day—she'd hoped it might make it easier for Lisa to face her grief and start to move on. Besides that, Stevie was afraid that if Lisa got in the habit of staying away from the stable, even for a little while, the habit just might stick now that Prancer was gone. And Stevie definitely didn't want that to happen. But now that Lisa was there, Stevie felt responsible for keeping her friend from sinking too deep into despair. "I feel for you, Carole, believe me," she said a little too loudly. "I've been grounded for so long I've practically forgotten what the mall looks like. Not to mention old what's-his-name—you know, my boyfriend . . ." She pretended to think hard for a moment. "Is it Bill? Or maybe Will."

Lisa chuckled, though Stevie couldn't help thinking it sounded a bit forced. "Don't worry. Even if you've forgotten Phil, I'm sure he hasn't come close to forgetting you," she joked weakly. "Besides, I'm sure your parents will unground you soon. It's been a while since the party."

Stevie sighed wistfully as she thought about her boyfriend, Phil Marsten. It really had been a long time since the two of them had been free to go to the movies or just hang out whenever they felt like it. Still, she was trying to look on the bright side. "Actually, I don't want to jinx myself or anything, but I think Mom and Dad are actually starting to ease up some. They said okay right away when I asked if I could come here to visit Belle today." She shrugged. "I mean, I'm definitely not totally off the most wanted list yet, but I can tell they're weakening. Losing their taste for cracking the whip. Before you know it, I'll be a free agent again."

Carole smiled slightly, and Stevie caught a faint twinkle in her dark eyes. "That's just like you, Stevie," Carole said. "Always the optimist." She checked her watch and her expression sobered again. "Um, listen, I'd better get going," she said quietly. "Dad's expecting me home pretty soon, and I still have to talk to Max. And I really want to visit with Samson a little bit first."

Stevie gulped. She had almost forgotten about Samson. "Okay," she said. "Lisa and I were just on our way out anyway. We already stuffed Belle so full of carrots she can hardly move." She paused. "Um, good luck. With Max, I mean."

"Thanks." Giving a listless half wave, Carole turned and headed for the stable aisle.

With a worried sigh, Stevie watched her walk away. When she returned her attention to Lisa, she saw that she was once again staring blankly into space.

"Poor Carole," Stevie said. "Can you believe all this happened? And right before her birthday, too."

Lisa blinked. "Her birthday," she repeated blankly. "I almost forgot about that. I mean, I remembered last week, but . . ." She cleared her throat. "It's tomorrow, isn't it? What are we going to do to celebrate?"

"I don't know," Stevie admitted. "Somehow I don't think the colonel's going to approve any kind of big blowout right now. He may not even let us come over and do the candle-on-a-cupcake thing." She shrugged. "At least you'll get to see her at school." Lisa and Carole both attended Willow Creek High, while Stevie attended Fenton Hall, a private school across town from the public school.

"Only between classes," Lisa reminded her. "We don't even have lunch together this year."

Stevie nodded. Like her, Carole was a junior, a year behind Lisa. "Well, I guess it's pretty much a given that this year won't go down in history as one of Carole's greatest birthdays or anything," she said, running a hand distractedly through her thick, dark blond hair. "Still, maybe we can think of some way to mark the occasion."

"Maybe." Lisa didn't sound too sure about that.

Stevie decided not to dwell on it. "Okay, time to motor," she said as brightly as she could. "I don't want to push my luck with Mom and Dad. I figure if I play the model prisoner for a few more days, they'll be ready to start talking parole. So are you ready to go? I'll drop you off."

"I think I'll stay for a few more minutes. There's something I want to do."

"Do you want me to stay, too?" Stevie asked. "I'm sure a few minutes won't totally blow my case with the 'rents."

Lisa knew that Stevie was trying to help, and she loved her for it. But she also knew that there was something she had to do now that even her best friends couldn't help her with. "Thanks," she said. "But you go ahead. I'll be okay."

Stevie looked a little doubtful, but she nodded. "Call me later, okay? I'm not promising the wardens will let me chat, but . . ."

Lisa nodded and said good-bye to her friend. As soon as Stevie had disappeared through the door, she turned and crossed the entryway, heading for the farther arm of the U-shaped stable aisle. She couldn't help noticing that Pine Hollow seemed quiet for a weekend morning, and she guessed that people were sleeping in after all the previous day's excitement. Several Pine Hollow riders had participated in a big horse show, and a lot of people had attended the show to cheer them on. Now Lisa was glad of the solitude—she wasn't in the mood for socializing. She walked down the aisle, following the familiar path to Prancer's stall. She did her best to prepare herself, but even so, it gave her a tiny jolt when she reached the door and saw that the stall was swept clean, the water bucket and hayrack empty, the overhead lightbulb switched off to conserve energy.

Grabbing the edge of the half door for support, Lisa forced herself to take a good long look at the empty stall. This was the sight she'd been dreading, the reason she had resisted at first when Stevie had turned up at her doorstep an hour earlier to drag her to Pine Hollow. As long as she didn't have to look at the vacated stall, she wouldn't really have to believe that it was true—that Prancer was gone. It was the sight that Lisa had tried not to imagine the entire time she was watching Stevie feed her own horse, Belle, pieces of carrot. But she hadn't been able to stop herself from remembering the dainty, precise way Prancer used to pick up individual carrot chunks from her own palm. Sometimes the mare had managed to work her way through a dozen pieces of carrot without doing more than brushing Lisa's hand with the whiskers on her lips.

She was totally different when it came to apples, though, Lisa thought with a wistful smile. *She used to slurp those up so fast I'd have horse slobber up to my shoulder by the time she was finished.*

Hardly aware of what she was doing, Lisa unlatched the stall door and slipped inside. The hard-packed dirt floor felt strange beneath her feet without its usual cushion of deep, soft straw. A few specks of dust floated in the beam of sunlight coming through the high, narrow window in the back wall.

Lisa reached out and touched the battered manger, the one that Prancer had eaten from every day of her life at Pine Hollow. She walked around the perimeter of the roomy stall, remembering the way the mare had nosed each corner of it whenever Lisa returned her after a ride, as if checking to make sure that everything was still as it should be.

Then Lisa sat down and leaned against the wall with her knees drawn up to her chest. Resting her chin on her knees, she allowed the memories to sweep over her and the tears to roll freely down her face.

TWO

"Left foot, please," Callie Forester said, tapping the bay gelding on the left foreleg. She smiled as he blinked twice, then slowly shifted his weight, raising his foot off the straw-covered floor. "Thank you, sir," she said, catching the horse's hoof and bending over it with her hoof pick. Windsor had a thoughtful, dignified way of doing things that always amused her. Callie had only been riding the big bay for a few days, but she had already grown fond of his quirks and his unique personality.

She was also grateful for the fact that he had a mind of his own and could sometimes be a challenge when he thought he was right and she was wrong. He was nowhere near as spirited as the horses Callie had been accustomed to riding at her old stable back on the West Coast. But he was a lot more exciting than reliable old Patch, the horse she'd been riding lately at Pine Hollow. Callie liked Patch—he was kind and patient

13

and steady—but she preferred a horse that kept her on her toes. In her chosen sport, endurance riding, a horse's personality was important. Callie had always had the best luck with vigorous horses who were willing to fight hard for every last mile out on the trail.

And Callie expected no less of herself. She had become a junior endurance champion by never giving up, by always wanting to be the best, and most of all by training hard every chance she got. For the past few years she had spent every possible minute out on the trail or in the ring, conditioning and training herself and her mounts, always looking forward to the next fifty- or hundred-mile race.

All that had changed soon after Callie's family had moved to Willow Creek, Virginia, the previous summer to be closer to her congressman father's office in Washington, D.C. Callie still found it hard to believe how completely her life had been transformed in a matter of seconds—as long as it took the car she was riding in to skid off the rain-slicked road in front of Pine Hollow, roll over, and tumble down a hill. The next thing Callie knew, she was in the hospital with residual brain damage, which translated into a right leg that wouldn't do what she wanted it to. Ever since, she had been doing all she could to get her old life and her old body back—putting her famous single-mindedness to work on the task of getting better. And she was so close. . . .

"I almost wish we weren't going back to Valley Vista next week," Callie confided to Windsor as she wedged her hoof pick under a stubborn clod of packed dirt. "I'm not sure it will do me any good to take such a long break from our therapeutic riding sessions. Especially now that I'm making some real progress."

That was only part of the reason she had mixed feelings about her family's Thanksgiving plans, though she didn't voice the other part aloud. As soon as her father had announced that the family would be returning to their hometown during the upcoming school vacation, Callie had immediately imagined what her old friends would say when they saw her. What they would think.

Callie's gaze wandered to the shiny metal crutches leaning against Windsor's hayrack. She sighed as she imagined how good it would feel to throw them out the stall's small window right then and there. It had been almost five months since the accident, and the last thing she felt like doing was discussing it over and over again. But, knowing her parents, she would encounter every person in Valley Vista by the time the week was over, and she dreaded the thought of their nosy

15

questions. She had moved on, and she wasn't the type of person who liked to dwell on the past.

"What do you think, mister?" she asked Windsor, lowering his hoof to the ground. "Do you think the old gang will believe me if I tell them crutches are all the rage here in Virginia?"

The horse's only reply was to turn his head slightly and blink at her sleepily, swiveling his ear to dislodge a pesky fly. But Callie already knew the answer to her own question. Her friends in Valley Vista would be perfectly polite to her face, no matter what she decided to tell them about what had happened. But behind her back was another story. She had already learned how deceitful people could be when her former best friend, Sheila, had written a tell-all article for the local newspaper after a visit with Callie and her family. That had also helped Callie to realize that some of her friendships back on the West Coast had been less than what she'd thought they were. The good part of that was that it made her appreciate the true friends she'd made in Willow Creek—Stevie, Carole, Lisa, Alex, Phil, and a few others. But it also made her sad to think about all the time she'd wasted on people who were only interested in getting close to her because of her well-known name or her blond hair and slender good looks.

I guess it's like Scott is always telling me, she

16

thought. *I've just got to deal. It's part of the territory when you belong to a well-known family. We're in the spotlight 24/7, and that's just the way it is.* She knew her brother was right about that, but that didn't mean she had to like it.

Callie did her best to push her restless thoughts out of her mind as she continued Windsor's grooming. Like most horses, the big bay enjoyed being fussed over, and it didn't take long for Callie to finish picking out his feet and brush the dirt and sweat out of his chocolate-brown coat. She cleaned his face, taking extra care with his ears, rubbing them for a few extra minutes and making the horse sigh with contentment.

Finally the big gelding was clean and comfortable. After dropping her tools in her grooming bucket, Callie gave Windsor one last pat. "There you go, mister," she said. "I'll see you *mañana,* okay?"

She turned away from the horse, preparing to leave the stall. Her crutches were just an arm's length away, and Callie started to reach for them automatically.

But then she hesitated. Taking a deep breath, she turned her gaze toward the stall door, just three or four steps away. Could she do it? She didn't know. But that only made her more determined to try.

She took a deep breath. *Left foot first,* she told herself.

Clenching her teeth, she focused on keeping her weaker right leg steady as she stepped off with her good leg. She wobbled slightly but stayed upright as her left foot hit the floor. Now came the hard part. Callie leaned farther forward, putting more of her weight on her left leg. Then she willed her right leg to move, swinging it slowly forward, bringing it even with the other leg and then past.

So far, so good, she thought with a burst of elation as her foot touched the floor.

But her joy was short-lived. As she shifted her weight forward again, she felt her weak leg buckle under the pressure and give way, the muscles refusing to move as she desperately tried to adjust her balance. She pitched forward, throwing out her hands just in time to avoid bumping her head on the front wall of the stall.

"Damn!" she cried, feeling hot tears of frustration spring to her eyes as she pulled herself up on the crossbeam of the stall door. "Damn, damn, *damn!*"

"Watch your language, sis," a familiar voice came from just outside the stall. "Windsor's at that impressionable age, you know."

Startled, Callie glanced up and saw her brother watching her over the stall's half door.

Feeling embarrassed, she blinked back her tears and frowned at him. "What are you doing here already?" she asked, hoping he hadn't guessed what she was up to. "I thought you weren't coming to pick me up for like another half hour."

Scott shrugged, a slightly sheepish expression on his handsome face. "Really?" he said, running a hand through his close-cropped brown hair. "I guess I must've spaced on the time. Sorry, don't mean to rush you. I can go wander around if you're not ready."

Callie was barely listening. Grabbing her crutches, she swung open the stall door and maneuvered herself into the stable aisle. Scott stepped aside to get out of her way, then reached over to latch the stall door, giving Windsor a pat as he did so.

"Forget it, I'm ready," Callie said, feeling rather out-of-sorts. She didn't like failing at something she set out to do, and she liked being caught failing even less, even by her own brother. "As long as you're here early, we might as well take off. I've got a ton of homework to do for tomorrow."

Scott nodded agreeably and kept pace with her as she headed down the aisle. "Me too," he said. "I wonder why teachers always feel the need to pile it on right before a holiday?"

"Who knows?" Callie said distractedly.

"Maybe you should start up a task force or something to study the problem."

Scott chuckled. He had recently been elected student body president of Fenton Hall. "Maybe I will," he said. "I think that's an issue the whole school could go for."

Callie didn't bother to answer. She paused to put her grooming bucket away, then resumed thinking about her failed experiment. She hadn't really tried walking without her crutches for the past week or so, and she was disappointed to discover that she still seemed to have a way to go before she would be ready to toss them for good.

But I still have almost a week before we leave for Valley Vista, she told herself, feeling her old determination creep back and take over again. *I can do a lot in the next week.* She glanced down at her crutches. *A whole lot.*

"Mayday, mayday," Scott muttered suddenly, nudging her shoulder and startling her out of her thoughts. He nodded slightly at the aisle ahead of them. "Desperate wannabe love slave at twelve o'clock."

Callie followed his gaze and saw a slightly pudgy, moon-faced guy hurrying toward them. She groaned under her breath. "Oh, man," she said. "Just what I *don't* need right now."

She felt slightly guilty for saying it. George Wheeler had been nothing but nice to her since they'd met. But she had never been quite comfortable with him since realizing that he had a major case of the hots for her. After she'd told him that she didn't see him that way, he'd agreed that they would just be friends, and at first Callie had tried to believe him. But lately she had to admit that she'd been kidding herself. George might say they were nothing but good buddies now, but it was painfully obvious that his feelings for her hadn't changed a bit.

"Callie!" George called eagerly, lifting one hand to wave. "Hi!"

"Hi," Callie called back weakly. She felt her hands clenching more tightly on the grips of her crutches. Sometimes she was tempted just to tell him to take a hike, to leave her alone and stop trying so hard to pretend to be Mr. Platonic. It wouldn't have been the first time she'd had to blow off a too-persistent suitor.

But George was different from most of the guys who pursued Callie. He was so sensitive, so nerdy and vulnerable. She just couldn't bring herself to nuke him that way. It would be like kicking a puppy.

George skidded to a stop in front of Callie, an eager grin revealing the deep dimples on his round, pink cheeks. "Callie," he said. "I thought you might be here. Did you finish your session?"

Callie opened her mouth to answer, but her

mind was a blank. Suddenly she wasn't sure she could do it anymore—she had no idea what to say to him to maintain their ridiculous charade. What was more, she didn't have the energy to try, not on top of her other worries. She blinked helplessly and glanced at her brother, sending him a mental plea for help. Fortunately, Scott caught her look. Shooting her a quick wink, he turned to the other guy with his most charming, most sincere friend-to-the-world smile.

"Yo, George, my man," he said breezily, reaching out to give him a hearty clap on the shoulder. "How's it going?"

"Hi, Scott," George said automatically, though his eyes never left Callie's face. "I'm fine. How are you?"

"In a hurry, unfortunately," Scott said in the smooth, pleasant tone that had won him the friendship of just about every person he'd ever met. "Wish we could stay and catch up, but Callie and I have to bail. Mom wants us home five minutes ago."

"Oh." The disappointment was plain on George's face, but he nodded politely. "Well, too bad. See you soon."

Callie breathed a sigh of relief, avoiding George's adoring gaze as her brother hustled her toward the exit.

———

"I hate to say it, big guy," Carole whispered to the black horse, running her hands down his sleek, muscular neck, "but I think I'd better get going. Dad will strangle me if I'm late."

She felt her tears rising again as she stepped back and looked at Samson. She blinked hard, willing herself not to start bawling. She would have plenty of time to cry over everything that had happened. Now she just wanted to get through the next few minutes without totally losing it.

She wasn't sure that was possible. Until the day before, she'd hoped that someday soon, Samson might belong to her for real. In some ways he had always belonged to her—he had held a special place in her heart since the day Carole and her friends had assisted with his foaling right there at Pine Hollow. From the moment she had first set eyes on the gangly black foal with the spirited expression in his dark eyes, Carole had known that he was something special.

Samson had done everything to prove her right. "You're a real champ, you know," she said softly, reaching forward to touch his black-velvet nose with her fingertips. "Yesterday, when the judge pinned the blue ribbon to your bridle? That was the best moment of my whole life." She paused for a moment, savoring the memory.

Even tinged as it was with the pain of everything else that had happened that day, she knew it was one she would always treasure.

Especially since it was just about all she would have left of Samson. From now on, someone else would be smiling proudly for the cameras as judges clipped ribbon after ribbon to the spirited gelding's bridle. After all, wasn't that why a famous Canadian rider had bought him from Max? Because he wanted a horse capable of winning at the highest levels? For a moment Carole found herself wishing that Samson wasn't the incredible athlete he was. That he didn't have an amazing talent for jumping, combined with the speed and fire and will to win that made him stand out even in a crowd of equine superstars.

But she couldn't quite make herself mean it. Samson wouldn't be Samson without those qualities. And she wouldn't change a hair on his hide, no matter what had happened.

"You're one of a kind, Samson," she told the horse softly, slipping her arms around his glossy neck for one last hug. "No matter how hard it is to say good-bye, I wouldn't trade one second of our time together. Knowing you—loving you— has taught me so much. . . ." Her voice drifted off as she closed her eyes and hugged him tight.

Samson stood quietly for a moment under her embrace. Then, restless, he snorted and tossed his head, dislodging her arms. Carole stepped back, knowing it was getting late. It was time to go.

I can't believe I'm never going to ride him again, she thought, drinking in the sight of the big black horse as she slowly backed toward the stall door. *I can't believe yesterday was the last time, and I didn't even know it. It's just so unfair. . . .*

Carole turned her back on the horse and reached for the latch. She heard him let out a curious snort behind her, but she couldn't bear to look back.

"Good-bye, Samson," she whispered, closing her eyes tight for a moment and clinging to the door for balance. She could almost feel her heart breaking.

As she let herself out of the stall, she automatically glanced up and down the stable aisle, keeping a lookout for Ben Marlow. Ben had worked full time at Pine Hollow since graduating from high school the year before. Among all the confusing things that had happened the previous day, perhaps most confusing of all was what had happened between Carole and Ben. After hearing that Max had sold Samson, Carole had needed some time to herself. She had retreated to a secluded patch of woods, with only the big black horse for company. A little while later, when she was almost cried out, Ben had found her hiding place. She had been grateful for his awkward attempts at offering comfort, especially since she knew that he was one of the few people who might truly understand how devastated she was to be losing Samson. The first thing she had ever noticed about Ben was the special rapport he had with horses. It was clear that he felt as strongly about his favorite creatures as she did, and they had formed a tentative friendship based on that. It wasn't anything like the kind of relationship Carole had with her other friends—Ben rarely confided anything personal about himself, and it was an unusual event when he seemed interested in hearing anything personal about anyone else, including Carole.

Then something had happened. As Carole had clung to Ben, taking strength from his understanding silence, he had looked down at her with an unreadable expression in his dark eyes. She had looked back at him. And somehow, Carole had found their faces moving closer almost imperceptibly. Before she quite realized what was happening, she had felt his lips meet hers, softly at first, then more insistently. She hadn't resisted—partly out of surprise, but mostly because she didn't want to resist. Suddenly all her grief-stricken thoughts about Samson had faded into the background, and her mind was filled with the moment, with kissing Ben. It felt so right somehow, as though it was meant to happen. . . .

But Ben had pulled away. Carole had been too startled and confused by what had happened to hear what he said as he hurried away, and she hadn't known quite what to think of the kiss, or her own feelings about it. With all the other distractions, she had managed to put the whole incident out of her mind—mostly.

Then, back at the stable, she and Ben had encountered each other in the aisle. That had brought back their moment together full force, and Carole had suddenly turned shy, wondering if Ben was feeling any of the same tentative, confused but hopeful emotions she was.

He hadn't left her in suspense for long. Instead of stopping to talk to her, he had brushed past with barely a grunt of greeting. His eyes had been cool and dismissive as they swept over her, and Carole had felt the one bright spot in the day, her one flicker of hope that her life wasn't completely in ruins, sputter and die.

Now all she could do was hope that she wouldn't have to face him today. She couldn't deal with that on top of everything else that was going on, and she could only pray that he would stay at home. Sunday was Ben's official day off, but more often than not he showed up at Pine Hollow anyway. The first few times, Max had tried to shoo him away. But apparently he had finally realized that his taciturn young employee was happiest being at the stable whether he was getting paid for it or not. Since then, Max had accepted Ben's presence on Sunday without complaint, though Carole had noticed that it wasn't long after that when Max announced he was so pleased with Ben's work that he was giving him a raise.

Maybe Ben won't show today, for once, she thought as she walked down the aisle toward Starlight's stall, not sure whether that would make her feel better or worse.

When she reached the stall and looked in, she saw that Starlight wasn't alone.

"Oh!" exclaimed the girl who was standing inside, feeding the gelding a bit of carrot. She blinked at Carole with wide, startled eyes. "Carole! Um, sorry, I hope you don't mind, I—"

"It's okay, Rachel." Carole hastened to reassure the younger girl. "I don't mind you stopping in to say hi to Starlight. I'm sure he appreciates the attention, too." Seventh-grader Rachel Hart was a member of Pine Hollow's intermediate riding class. Recently, when Carole had decided she wanted to sell Starlight and buy Samson, Rachel was one of the people she'd approached. Rachel had been thrilled at the idea of owning the talented bay gelding. But her parents weren't convinced that she was ready for her own horse, so she had been forced to tell Carole that she was out of the running.

"Okay," Rachel said, still looking a little embarrassed about being caught. "Thanks. I just really felt like I needed to come here and hang out with him for a while. It's been kind of weird around here lately, you know?"

"I know." Even though she was glad that Starlight was still hers, Carole felt sorry for the younger girl. Not only had Rachel been disappointed in her dream to buy Starlight, but she was probably really sad about Prancer's death, too. For the past year, she had been one of the mare's most regular riders after Lisa.

"By the way," Rachel said shyly, "congratulations on your ribbon yesterday. You were really great. And, um, sorry about the other stuff."

Carole didn't have to ask which "other stuff" Rachel meant. She was sure that the news of her grounding was all over the stable by now.

"Thanks," she told Rachel, shifting her gaze to her horse so that the younger girl wouldn't see the pain in her eyes. As she watched Starlight lower his head to snuffle curiously at Rachel's shoulder, Carole suddenly had an idea. "Hey, listen," she said. "Are you going to be around for the holidays? You know, Thanksgiving and

Christmas? Will you be in Willow Creek, or does your family go away somewhere?"

Rachel shrugged. "I guess we'll be here. All my relatives are coming down to our house this year for Thanksgiving—it's my mom's turn to cook. And we don't usually go anyplace for Christmas."

"Great," Carole said. "Then how would you feel about taking care of Starlight for me while I'm, um, away? You could ride him for your lessons, and that way your folks won't have to pay for you to ride one of Max's horses. In exchange, you could make sure he gets enough exercise, keep up with his tack and grooming—you know, the works. What do you say?"

Rachel's eyes lit up. "Really?" she said. "I'd love that! Are you sure you want me to do it?"

"Trust me, you'll be doing me a favor," Carole assured her, relieved that Rachel seemed so excited about the idea. Knowing that Starlight had an enthusiastic, responsible young caretaker would make Carole worry a little less about him during her grounding. "So do we have a deal?"

"Definitely!" Rachel stuck out her hand.

Carole smiled and shook it firmly. "Good. You can start right away if you want. I'll clear everything with Max before I leave here today."

"Cool!" Rachel patted Starlight on the neck, looking thrilled. "This is the perfect way to prove to my parents that I'm ready for my own horse." She glanced at Carole shyly. "I mean, even if you're not planning to sell Starlight anymore, um . . ."

Carole took that to mean that Rachel already knew all about Samson's departure, too. Pine Hollow wasn't a big place, and any piece of juicy gossip tended to spread like a barn fire. Carole blushed slightly as she thought about Ben. At least that was one thing the younger riders weren't buzzing about. She hadn't told a soul about the kiss yet, not even her best friends. And Ben wasn't exactly the type to spill his guts about anything to anyone. "I understand," she told Rachel, who still looked a little anxious. "It will show your parents that you can handle the responsibility."

Rachel looked relieved. "Right. So is there anything special I should know?"

"Not too much," Carole said. "Starlight's a pretty easy keeper. Normal grain ration, no grooming issues. But he's due for new shoes in a couple of weeks, so you'll have to remember to get him on the farrier's schedule. And if you don't keep after him about his half-halts, he gets lazy about it quick, so don't let him get away with being sloppy even once. And I was sort of planning to focus on ground training for the next couple of weeks, but if you want to work on jumping . . ."

Rachel didn't interrupt as Carole reeled off everything else she could think of. At the end, the younger girl just nodded. "Thanks, Carole," she said. "I won't let you down. I'll take good care of him for you, I swear."

Carole smiled wanly. "I know you will," she said. "And I'm the one who should be thanking you. I'll go tell Max about our arrangement in a minute, okay? Right now I just want to, um, you know, say good-bye. You know."

Rachel nodded and slipped out of the stall, leaving Carole alone with Starlight. Carole turned and looked at her horse, automatically moving her hands up to rub his face as he nosed at her. The sight of the big six-pointed star splashed on his mahogany face was so familiar that it was almost painful. She found it hard to believe that she had almost sent him away forever. At least that hadn't actually happened. At least that was one thing that had gone her way lately.

"And at least now I won't have to worry about you while I'm away, boy," she said softly, resting her head against the horse's warm, solid neck. "That's one thing I can be thankful for."

THREE
3

Stevie had her head buried in the refrigerator, searching for a snack, when she heard the back door slam and then felt someone poke her in the side. "Yo," a familiar voice said. "Leave some food in there for the rest of us, okay?"

Stevie turned and rolled her eyes at her twin brother, Alex. "Look who's talking, Oink-Boy," she said. "With the way you scarf down everything in sight, it's practically a miracle the rest of us get anything to eat at all." She was only half kidding. Alex had shot up almost a foot in the past year and a half, and he was still just as thin and wiry as ever, despite the fact that he ate enough to feed a small nation, as their mother liked to put it—or that he ate like a horse and a half, as Stevie was more likely to say.

Alex ignored her insult. "So did you get Lisa to the stable today?" he asked.

Stevie nodded, turning serious. She liked to give all three of her brothers a hard time when—

ever the mood struck her, but she rarely teased Alex about his relationship with Lisa. It had been a big surprise to Stevie when her twin and her best friend had fallen for each other. She had adjusted to the idea since then—she loved them both and thought it was wonderful that they had found happiness with each other—though at odd moments she still found herself amazed that their romance actually worked when they were so fundamentally different in so many ways. She supposed that was an example of opposites attracting.

"She came along," Stevie replied, leaning back into the refrigerator long enough to pluck out a plastic container of leftover chicken. "Actually, I left her there. She wanted to be alone."

Alex pursed his lips somberly. He had only taken up riding after he'd started dating Lisa, so he didn't have quite the same attachment to the horses at Pine Hollow as Lisa, Carole, and she did. But he knew that Prancer had been very important to Lisa, and that meant he was concerned about his girlfriend now. "Do you think she's going to be okay?"

"Sure. We just have to give her some time." Stevie sat down at the kitchen table and peeled the lid off the container. "I mean, she got through her parents' divorce, right? She'll get through this."

Alex nodded. He sat down across the table from Stevie and leaned his chin on one hand. "I guess you're right," he agreed. "I only wish there was more I could do to help her. Or at least that I could be there—you know, as in actually *there*—for her more." He sighed noisily. "Being grounded really bites, you know?"

"I know. I've practically forgotten what Phil looks like." Stevie had spent most of the previous day at the horse show with her boyfriend, but she chose to ignore that fact in light of the much longer time they'd been separated by her grounding. It wasn't easy—they had been together for a long time, and Stevie really missed seeing Phil whenever she wanted, kissing him whenever the mood struck her. . . . "Besides that," she added, "he's been dealing with this A.J. situation pretty much on his own."

Reaching for a piece of chicken, Alex glanced at Stevie, his hazel eyes reflecting curiosity and concern. "Yeah," he said. "I was just wondering what was up with A.J. lately. I meant to ask Phil yesterday, but the scene at the show was so crazy I totally forgot. What's the latest?"

Stevie frowned as she thought about the answer to that question. A.J. McDonnell had been Phil's best friend for as long as Stevie had known him. For most of that time A.J. had been a friendly, happy-go-lucky guy with a quick sense of humor and boundless enthusiasm for fun. But a couple of months earlier he had suddenly started acting like a completely different person—sometimes sullen and withdrawn, sometimes manic and edgy, always unpredictable. Even after his friends learned that A.J. had discovered that he was adopted and that his parents had withheld the fact from him, Stevie still had trouble believing that a person could change so drastically overnight.

"Phil says he doesn't seem to be dealing any better," Stevie said, watching her brother stuff most of a chicken wing into his mouth. "Did Lisa tell you how she ran into him at that college bar?"

Alex chewed and swallowed, then nodded. "She said he was chugging beers in a big way."

"And that was just a few days after Phil caught him spiking his soda with vodka," Stevie reminded him. She drummed her fingers on the table. "I hate to sound like an Afterschool Special here, but it's really starting to sound like A.J.'s got a problem."

"I think you're right," Alex agreed. "I mean, at first I thought he was just acting out—you know, sort of trying to get back at his parents for never telling him he was adopted." He leaned back and tossed the bones from his chicken wing into the trash can by the back door. "But it's getting way out of control."

"I know," Stevie said. "The question is, what do we do about it?"

Alex licked grease off his fingers and shrugged. "Who knows? I guess we should have watched more of those Afterschool Specials."

Stevie was about to reply when the back door swung open and their father walked in. Seeing the two of them at the table, he hurried toward them. "Hi," he said briskly. "Listen, I just came from your mother's office. The lawyer who was supposed to host this month's partners' meeting just came down with bronchitis, and your mom's boss volunteered us to take his place." He rubbed his forehead, looking harried. "So we're going to have a whole houseful of lawyers here on Wednesday night, and somehow between now and then we have to figure out what to feed them. Can you two help us out by making yourselves scarce that day?"

Stevie feigned shock. "You mean leave the house—while we're grounded?" she said with a loud gasp. "But—But—I don't understand!"

"Very funny, Stevie." Mr. Lake rolled his eyes. "We'll be having an early dinner here, then heading out to a lecture over at the community college. So you can plan to be back home around six-thirty or thereabouts to start your homework and chores. Now, do you think you can manage that or not?"

"We can manage, Dad." Alex spoke up quickly, before Stevie could say another word. "We can manage just fine. Thanks."

Mr. Lake nodded. "Naturally, we'd appreciate any help you could give us in the next two and a half days to whip the house into shape."

"Naturally," Stevie said. "We're on it."

"Thanks." Mr. Lake glanced at his watch, then headed out toward the living room.

When he was gone, Alex grinned. "Hey, how about that? We were just talking about wanting more time with Lisa and Phil. And here it is, just dropped in our laps. What are the odds?"

Stevie shot her twin a sidelong glance as she jumped to her feet. "I don't know. Probably about the same as the odds of you beating me to the phone right now."

The office door was open when Carole got there, so she knocked softly on the frame. "Hi, Max," she said. "Do you have a minute?"

Max looked up from some paperwork. "Sure, Carole. Come on in." Dropping his pen, he leaned back in his chair and rubbed his eyes. "Actually, I could use your help if you're not too busy with other work. I just started updating the boarding records, and I think you're the only person around this place who can decipher Denise's handwriting." He chuckled wryly. "I don't think Denise herself can understand it half the time."

Carole forced a smile. Denise McCaskill was Max's daytime stable manager. Her brisk, energetic personality carried over into her handwriting, which was often so hurried that it was barely legible. Carole and everyone else at the stable had teased Denise for years about her jagged scrawl.

But at the moment, Max's words only reminded Carole of what she was there to do. She was there to confess something sordid and bad and humiliating to one of the people she respected most in the world. One of the people who, until today, she'd been sure respected her a lot, too.

She glanced around the stable office. As usual, it was in a state of controlled chaos. One of the file drawers was open, and Carole could see the names of Pine Hollow's boarders and their owners typed on the top tab of each hanging file— *Belle, S. Lake; Country Doctor, A. Barry; Joyride, G. Wheeler; Pinky, J. Phillips; Romeo, P. Giacomin; Starlight, C. Hanson* . . . Averting her eyes quickly from her own name, Carole took in the cluttered desktop. A hoof gauge was holding down a stack of invoices from the feed company, and nearby, a bridle with a broken buckle awaited repair. Books on horsemanship and equine health overflowed the shelves that lined the walls, and the door leading to the tack room was propped open with a large plastic tub of antibacterial ointment. Carole couldn't see the lost-and-found box under the desk or her spare pair of stable shoes in the employees' closet, but she knew they were there. It was all so familiar and comforting that she didn't know how she was going to stand being away.

Taking a deep breath, she plunged right in. "I don't really know how to say this," she said, her voice already starting to shake a little. Clearing her throat, she went on, avoiding Max's direct, questioning gaze. "Um, I have something to—to confess. Something pretty horrible."

Max put his arms on the desk and leaned forward. "Yes?"

"It's nothing to do with the stable," Carole said hastily. She reached up and twisted a strand of curly black hair around her finger, an old nervous habit. "It happened at school. I—I sort of cheated. On a test."

"Sort of?" Max repeated.

Carole bit her lip. "Not sort of," she said in a tiny voice. She could feel her face growing hot. "I did. I cheated. It was stupid and wrong, and I regretted it the second I did it. But I was afraid if

I didn't do it, my grades would slip, and I wouldn't be allowed to ride here anymore." One of Max's strictest stable rules was that all school-age riders had to maintain at least a C average.

"I see." Max's voice was solemn. "Is that all you have to say?"

"Not exactly." Carole felt awful. "Um, see, the reason I'm telling you this now is that Dad just found out about it—yesterday at the horse show."

"I see," Max said again.

Carole gulped. "He was really mad—he *is* really mad. He—He—He . . ." She paused and swallowed hard, trying to stop her voice from shaking. "He grounded me. Until New Year's. I'm not allowed to ride here anymore, and I can't take care of Starlight myself—but don't worry, Rachel already said she'd do it if it's okay with you, and that way he'll get plenty of exercise while I'm away. Oh. And also, I—I have to quit my job."

Max was silent for a long, long moment. Finally he coughed. "I see," he said once more. "Well, I won't say I'm not shocked by this, Carole. But I appreciate your honesty. And I can certainly understand your father's position."

"I'm really sorry," Carole said in a tiny voice. "I know this means there's going to be more work for everyone else around here. I've totally messed up."

Max rubbed his chin. "I'm sure we can make do for a little while now that the horse show is over," he said. "And I was thinking about taking on another full-time hand after the holidays anyway. This way, I'll just need to find someone a little sooner. Then, after New Year's . . ."

Carole could hardly believe her ears. Glancing up cautiously, she saw that Max looked thoughtful but not angry. "You—You mean I can have my job back when my grounding is over?"

"Of course." Max looked surprised that she had even asked. "You're one of my hardest workers, Carole. Sometimes I wonder how I used to run this place before you signed on."

Carole couldn't help blushing slightly, but she also smiled. Max's kind words were the first bit of good news she'd had all day. The stable owner could be stern with his students or his employees anytime he thought they weren't doing their best. But Max clearly sensed that Carole already felt as awful as she could possibly feel about what she'd done. And he wasn't going to do anything to make her feel worse.

He was being so nice that Carole almost worked up the nerve to ask when Samson was leaving. Almost. But Max still didn't know that she had dreamed of buying the big black gelding herself, and she was afraid that her face or her voice would give her away. And she couldn't stand that. She couldn't face Max's pity on top of everything else. Instead, she brought up her agreement with Rachel again and they discussed the details briefly.

When that last bit of business was out of the way, Carole stood up, reluctant to leave the office. "Well—thanks," she said awkwardly. "Um, just so you know, I spoke to the farrier on Friday about Comanche's shoes, and he's going to call back when he knows his schedule for the week. And I never got around to fixing the latch on the schooling ring gate before the show, so I guess someone else will have to do that. And the feed—"

"It's all right, Carole," Max said gently. "Go. We'll take care of it. Don't worry about us."

Carole nodded, her throat suddenly tight, as if she might cry. Blinking hard, she turned away and walked toward the office door. This was it. It was time to go. Leaving the stable at the end of the day had never been easy for her—there was always one more horse to look in on, one more chore to do.

But this was different, and much worse. Because this time, she knew she wouldn't be back for a long, long while.

FOUR

The next morning Lisa stared at herself in the bathroom mirror. "Whoever invented Mondays should be shot," she muttered, rubbing a stray spot of mascara from the corner of her eyelid. Her delicate, high-cheekboned face stared back at her from the mirror, looking perfectly normal except for a slight frown. Almost as if nothing unusual had happened over the weekend. With a sigh, she turned away from her reflection and headed for the door.

At least I have one thing to look forward to this week, she reminded herself, thinking of her upcoming date with Alex. It had seemed like a miracle when he'd called to say that his parents were lifting his grounding for one day. Lisa couldn't wait. Their relationship hadn't exactly been what she would call smooth for the past few months, but she was sure they could get it back on track as soon as this grounding business was behind them. This date would be the perfect way to get started. Besides that, she knew she could count on Alex not only to sympathize with her in grieving over Prancer, but also to do his very best to take her mind off her sadness for a little while.

When she entered the kitchen, she found that she had it to herself and guessed that her mother was sleeping late. Lisa wasn't especially disappointed about that. She didn't feel like facing anyone at the moment, least of all her mother.

Mrs. Atwood had never been what Lisa would call a happy person. She had always been very concerned with appearances, which meant she'd been generally discontented with her family's comfortable middle-class existence. Lisa didn't know how much that attitude had to do with her father's walking out several years earlier, but the divorce had left her mother more bitter and depressed than Lisa could have imagined.

Things had gotten slightly better a month or so earlier when Mrs. Atwood had started dating a fellow employee at the clothing store where she worked as an assistant manager. She had been a lot happier since then—almost giddy, in fact. Her constant sniping about Lisa's father's betrayal had stopped, and she had started taking an interest in life again. That was the good news. The bad news, as far as Lisa was concerned, was her mother's choice of boyfriend, a twenty-five-year-old college sophomore named Rafe. Lisa had to admit that Rafe was good-looking in a languid, careless sort of way, with sleepy, cocoa-brown eyes and thick, shoulder-length dark hair. But his personality rubbed her the wrong way. He was a little too casual, a little too self-satisfied. Also, Lisa couldn't shake the growing concern that he was a lot less serious about her mother than she was about him. And that he knew it and didn't really care.

Pouring herself a glass of orange juice, Lisa did her best not to think about Rafe. With any luck her mother would come to her senses soon, before she got hurt. In the meantime, though, there was another problem to worry about. Whenever Mrs. Atwood wasn't gushing about her latest date with Rafe, she was harassing Lisa about her decision to attend Northern Virginia University, a local college, the following year.

Both of Lisa's parents had known that NVU was on the list of schools she was applying to, but when she'd been accepted early, she had decided all on her own to send back the form saying she would go there. By the time her mother and father found out, it was a done deal. And for some reason both of them seemed to think that Lisa had made a horrible mistake, even though she kept trying to explain that she'd given her choice a lot of serious thought. They just didn't seem interested in hearing what she had to say about the matter. That was why Lisa hadn't told a soul when she'd decided the night before to withdraw her applications to several other schools and throw away the blank application forms for two or three more. She'd just done it. That way nobody—not her parents, not her school guidance counselor, nobody—would be able to pressure her into changing her mind.

Lisa dropped a couple of slices of bread into the toaster and drummed her fingers on the counter as she waited for the toast to pop. The whole college shebang seemed pretty minor now compared to what had happened the day before. Intellectually, though, Lisa knew that it would all come back into focus once she'd had a chance to get used to the idea that Prancer was gone. Even if just at the moment it felt as though nothing could break through the fog of sadness that surrounded her.

Lisa had just taken her first bite of toast when she heard footsteps on the stairs. She braced herself, hoping her mother would have the sensitivity to avoid starting another argument about college this morning but knowing that the chances were slim.

"Good morning, Lisa dear," Mrs. Atwood sang out as she entered, wrapped in a silky red robe that Lisa recognized as an old Mother's Day gift from her father.

Lisa couldn't answer. She had just spotted Rafe slouching into the kitchen after her mother, twenty-four hours' worth of dark stubble on his angular chin and her older brother's ancient terry-cloth robe loosely tied around his waist. "Yo," he said with a yawn, lazily scratching his neck. "How's it going, Lisa?"

Lisa's jaw dropped. For a long moment, she couldn't respond. She just stared, hardly believing this scene was real and not some kind of demented nightmare. It was bad enough that the two of them were together at all—having dinner with each other practically every night, calling each other repulsive pet names, sucking face right in front of Lisa or whoever happened to be watching. Now he was spending the night at the house, too? It was too much—Lisa just couldn't compute the situation at the moment. Not now, when everything else was already so horrible.

Finally she found her voice again. "I've got to go," she blurted out, pushing her chair back so quickly that it almost toppled over. Before her mother or Rafe could respond, she raced out of the kitchen, leaving her breakfast behind.

"Could you pass the sugar please, Carole?" Colonel Hanson said, pouring himself a fresh cup of coffee from the pot in the center of the table.

Carole did as her father asked, not quite daring to meet his eyes. She couldn't stand the way he looked at her now—as if everything had changed between them, as if he saw her in a whole different way than he had before Saturday. Carole and her father had always been close, and they had only grown closer when Carole's mother had died of cancer years earlier. Carole had always loved their special relationship. Now she was afraid that, in one misguided moment, she had ruined all that forever.

Colonel Hanson cleared his throat. "Listen, Carole," he said. "I don't want you to think that I've forgotten it's your birthday today. But I also don't want to smile and sing and pretend everything is fine when it's not."

Carole blinked. With everything that had happened, she had almost forgotten her birthday herself. "Oh," she said. "My birthday. Right."

"Still," Colonel Hanson said, leaning over and reaching under the table, "I do have a few gifts I'd already wrapped up for you. So I guess you might as well go ahead and open them." He set a shopping bag on the table and pushed it toward her.

"Okay." Carole felt slightly nauseated. Would her father ever look at her normally again? Or would his face always wear that new, wary, disappointed expression when he met her eye?

She took the shopping bag and reached inside. The first and largest package, wrapped in pony-print paper, contained a new dark green turnout rug with Starlight's name embroidered on it in block letters. "Wow," Carole said. "Thanks, Dad. It's really nice."

Wow is right, she thought as she carefully folded the heavy green cloth and set it on the table. *Just imagine if I'd gone ahead and sold Starlight like I'd planned. Then what would I have done with this?*

She returned her attention to the shopping bag. There were two more packages inside. Carole unwrapped them quickly, revealing a pair of nice winter riding gloves and a brand-new book by a well-known horse trainer.

Setting the two gifts on top of the folded turnout rug, she smiled tentatively at her father. "Thanks, Dad," she said softly.

He nodded and took a sip of his coffee. "You're welcome," he replied, not really returning her smile. He glanced at his watch. "Now, hurry and finish your breakfast. It's almost time for you to leave for school. You want to get there a little early today, remember, so you have plenty of time to talk to your teacher."

Carole nodded. How could she forget? Her father had made it excruciatingly clear that he expected her to spill her guts to Ms. Shepard, her history teacher, as soon as humanly possible. Carole forced a few more spoonfuls of cereal down her throat, then carried her bowl to the sink and dumped the rest down the garbage disposal. She didn't have much of an appetite.

As she entered the school building a little while later, Carole felt like an unwanted, broken-down old nag walking to the slaughterhouse. After a quick stop at her locker, she took a deep breath and headed down the hall toward her history classroom. There was no sense in putting it off any longer.

Ms. Shepard was bent over some papers when Carole knocked softly on the door frame. "Excuse me," Carole said to the teacher. "Um, could I talk to you for a minute?"

"Carole," Ms. Shepard said, glancing up. "I had a feeling I might be seeing you this morning. Come right in. Just let me finish marking this quiz, or I'll never remember where I left off. It will just be a moment."

"Sure." Carole was thankful that Ms. Shepard didn't have homeroom duty. It would have been even worse to make her confession in front of a room full of eavesdropping classmates. Still, she knew it wasn't going to be easy to say what she had to say even in front of an empty classroom.

As the teacher quickly ran her pen down the paper in front of her, Carole's gaze kept wandering to her own seat. She could almost see herself sitting there even now, bending over her backpack and hurriedly flipping pages in her history book, looking up the answers she'd needed to pass that test. It hadn't really seemed as though she were making a choice at the time, but now she saw that she had. She had made the wrong choice, and she was paying for it in a big way.

Ms. Shepard finished her grading and put the paper aside, looking up at Carole again. "All right, there we go," she said, pushing her hair out of her face. "Now, what do you have to say to me this morning, my dear?"

Carole gulped and tried to focus. "I—I have something to tell you," she said as steadily as she could. Then she launched into her now familiar confession.

Ms. Shepard's kind face grew stern as Carole spoke. By the time Carole finished, the teacher was shaking her head grimly.

"Well, well," Ms. Shepard said severely, leaning forward with her elbows on her desk. "I have to say that I'm shocked, Carole. Of course I know now that you were being untruthful when you told me your father was ill to get me to give you that retest. Your father and I figured that out when we ran into each other at the horse show on Saturday." She shook her head slowly. "But I had no idea about the rest of it. This is a very serious matter."

Carole nodded miserably and shifted her weight from one foot to the other. Now that the dreaded confession was over, she felt oddly deflated. "I know," she said. "I'm sorry. I don't know what got into me. I was just so worried about flunking again. I mean, if my grade slipped too much, I wouldn't be able to ride anymore, and, well . . ."

Ms. Shepard blinked. "Oh," she said. "So that's what drove you to this. Horses."

"Yes," Carole said in a voice that was little more than a whisper. "I'm really sorry about what I did. But riding is really important to me, and I guess for a second there I kind of lost my head. You know, when I thought I might not be able to do it anymore." She grimaced. "And now I can't do it anymore anyhow, at least for now, because of what I did. When he found out about this, my dad banned me from the stable."

"I see." Ms. Shepard was silent for a moment, her frank hazel eyes studying Carole's face. "Well. Now I guess it's my turn to figure out what to do about this. It's a tough one, Carole—

mostly because I know you've never done anything like this before. Right?"

"I haven't," Carole agreed hastily. "I swear, I really haven't. I've never even *thought* about cheating before."

Ms. Shepard ran one hand through her loose brown curls, which Carole noticed were laced with strands of gray. "Yes, well, I wish you hadn't thought of it this time, either," the teacher said. "But I appreciate how difficult it was for you to come forward and be so honest with me. I have to commend you for that."

Carole wasn't sure she deserved any praise—after all, she never would have told if her father hadn't stumbled onto the secret. But she appreciated Ms. Shepard's gentle words nonetheless. "Thanks," she whispered.

Ms. Shepard smiled briefly, then turned serious again. "All right, then. What are we going to do about this?" She glanced down at her grade book, which was in its usual place at one corner of her desk. "The thing is, you have brought your grade up since then—it seems like a shame to give you a zero for that test and ruin your average."

Carole held her breath. It hadn't occurred to her until now that she could actually end up flunking history for this marking period. If that happened, she could kiss Pine Hollow good-bye for a lot longer than six weeks—great worker or not, Max wasn't going to bend his rules for her.

Ms. Shepard was tapping her pen thoughtfully against her cheek. "I think I have another idea, though," she said. "Instead of wasting your time with a lot of detention, why don't we try to be constructive about this? I think the best way to do that would be for you to write a research paper on the material covered on that test. Twenty pages. Footnotes. Due in three weeks. How does that sound?"

"It sounds great!" Carole exclaimed without thinking. "Um, I mean, thank you. That seems fair."

A hint of a smile flitted across the teacher's face. "All right, then," she said. "Three weeks. You can take a day or two to think about topics, and we'll discuss that when you're ready. Oh, but of course I'm going to have to report this to Dr. Durbin." Ms. Shepard looked slightly apologetic. "Even though it's your first offense, it's school policy to report every case of cheating."

Carole winced. She really hadn't thought past this talk with Ms. Shepard to imagine that anyone else would have to get involved. She certainly hadn't supposed that she might have to face Dr. Durbin, the school's vice principal.

Yikes, she thought. *Dr. Durbin is supposed to*

be a killer when it comes to stuff like this. With the way my luck's been going lately, Dr. Durbin will probably suspend me. Maybe even expel me. She cringed at the thought. *I'm sure Dad would just love that.*

FIVE

Callie kicked her backpack under her chemistry lab table and leaned her crutches against the table. Resting her weight on her arms, she pushed herself up onto the battered wooden stool, teetering slightly as the stool's uneven legs tilted her to one side.

"Are you okay?" George was already moving toward her. "Let me help you."

"I'm okay," Callie said quickly, regaining her balance and holding up a hand to keep George back. "It's under control. Really."

George didn't look entirely convinced, but he nodded and lowered himself back onto his own stool. "Hey, just one more week until Thanksgiving vacation," he commented cheerfully. "So what are your plans for next week when we're off? I guess I'll probably see you a lot at the stable, huh?"

"Afraid not," Callie replied quickly. She might have mixed feelings about her family's upcoming trip, but one thing was for sure—she was glad to be getting some distance from George for a little while. Maybe once he wasn't in her face all the time she could figure out how to deal with him. "Didn't I tell you? We're going back to Valley Vista for the whole week." She shrugged and smiled. "You know—Turkey Day with the constituents."

"Oh." Disappointment was plain on George's round face. "That's too bad."

Callie decided it would be best not to acknowledge that George looked positively crushed about her departure. To cover for them both, she jumped in to steer the conversation to more neutral ground. "Yes, good old Valley Vista," she said quickly. "I haven't been back there since we moved here, you know. It will be good to see the old gang again, check out the hot spots in town and see what's changed. I still have some relatives nearby—second cousins and a couple of great-aunts and stuff—so that will be nice, too."

"But won't you miss your therapeutic riding?" George asked. "I mean, won't it set you back, missing a whole week?"

Callie shrugged. "I'm sure I'll probably do some riding at my old stable," she said. "It's not quite as big as Pine Hollow, but my coach there was really good, and there are a couple of amazing horses I used to use to compete. It will be nice to see everyone again. Anyway, my leg is really a lot stronger now—I'm thinking about getting back to some endurance training soon."

"Really?" George's disappointed expression faded slightly, replaced by a look of interest. "Like what? I have to admit, I don't know that much about endurance riding. What kind of training do you do, anyway?"

Callie didn't particularly feel like discussing her training plans and goals with George. But she figured it was a much safer topic than plenty of others she could think of. "Well, a lot of being a good endurance rider is just being a good rider, period. And first I'll have to get back to that point. I have to make sure my body is strong enough, that I'm back in shape."

George was gazing at her intently, nodding. He was a very accomplished rider himself, so he already knew everything she'd just said. But she never would have guessed that from his rapt expression. "That makes sense," he said. "What else?"

Callie shrugged. "Well, I've already been working on my balance, of course," she said. "I mean, it was hard at first because my whole right side was pretty messed up. And you know how important balance is."

George nodded again. "Of course. And it

must be tough when you have to retrain half of your body."

It would have been an innocuous comment from just about anyone else. But Callie couldn't help wincing at hearing George talk about her body. She didn't like to consider that he might have been thinking about her body—weak right side or otherwise—quite a lot. To hide her agitation, she kept talking.

"Anyway," she said quickly, "lately I've been changing the length of my stirrups during my rides. That's something I do all the time when I'm in training because it helps strengthen all different muscles. Like I usually shorten the stirrups when I'm going to be doing a lot of downhill riding, because it's good for my knees and ankles."

"Interesting," George said, glancing down at Callie's legs beneath her khaki skirt.

Callie resisted the urge to tug her hem lower. *What's wrong with me?* she wondered. *George isn't exactly, well, Duke Elkin.* She almost smiled at that. She hadn't thought about Duke for months. He was a guy she'd dated briefly the year before, back in Valley Vista. She had been taken in by his dark, hulking good looks and his aggressive pursuit of her, but she'd dumped him as soon as she got to know him a little better—

especially his propensity for groping her friends whenever he saw an opportunity.

"Callie?" George said.

With a start, Callie realized she had fallen silent while thinking about Duke's roving hands. "Oh!" she said, glancing quickly at George. "Um, what was I saying? Oh yeah, I'll probably start doing more focused ground exercises, like to stretch my tendons and loosen up my ankles and stuff like that. And then when I'm ready, it will be time to start developing one of Max's horses so that I can aim toward entering a few easy races a few months down the road. We'll need to start with some basic ground training— stuff like neck stretches, maybe a little work with the chambon, and then on to schooling in the ring and out on the trail. I'll probably ask Max to help me decide which horse to use, but so far Barq seems like the best choice—he's an Arabian, so he's got a lot of natural endurance. And even though he has kind of a short stride, he'd probably do pretty well after some conditioning. Diablo or Rusty might have some possibilities, too, though I haven't ridden them myself yet so it's hard to say for sure. Of course, eventually I'll want to start shopping around for a real competition horse of my own. . . ."

As she spoke, Callie was aware that George was hanging on every pointless word that came out of her mouth, but she couldn't seem to stop herself from babbling on and on. It was a relief when their chemistry teacher came in and clapped her hands to begin class.

Callie clamped her mouth shut and sank down in her seat. *Get a grip, babe,* she told herself irritably. *Just chill. You're going to have to figure out a way to deal with George without coming down with a terminal case of diarrhea of the mouth every time you have to talk to him.*

She shook her head, feeling annoyed with herself. Maybe her week in Valley Vista would give her some much-needed perspective on what she was beginning to think of as the George Problem.

Carole was at lunch when the dreaded announcement finally came. "Attention, please," the PA speaker blared. "Will Carole Hanson please report to Dr. Durbin's office immediately? That's Carole Hanson to Dr. Durbin's office."

Carole's tuna sandwich suddenly turned to sawdust in her mouth. Swallowing with an effort, she quickly stuffed the rest of the sandwich back into her lunch bag and stood up, carefully avoiding the curious gazes of the students seated nearby.

"Yo, Hanson. What's the Durbinator want

with you?" called a guy from Carole's computer class who was sitting a few seats down.

Carole shrugged and smiled weakly. She was too nervous to come up with any kind of answer. But she could feel the curious gazes following her as she hurried toward the cafeteria door.

The halls outside were deserted. All the juniors and freshmen were in the cafeteria having lunch, while the seniors and sophomores were safely in their fifth-period classrooms. Carole could hear her footsteps echoing in the empty hallway as she passed the auditorium and rounded the corner toward the office. For one crazy second she was tempted to turn and race down the hall, straight out the double doors at the far end. If she kept running, she could be at Pine Hollow in a matter of minutes. She wouldn't bother with a saddle—she would just throw a bridle on Samson and clip a lead rope to Starlight's halter. Then the three of them would ride off into the rarely traveled wilds of the state forest, not returning until the world had turned right side up again. . . .

Carole sighed, shaking off the daydream. It was foolish to think she could just ride away from her problems. *After all, I brought them on myself,* she thought. *At least that's what Dad keeps telling me.* Glancing ahead, she saw that she was almost at the office. Taking a deep breath, she stepped forward and pushed open the clear glass door, which made a little bell tinkle overhead.

The school secretary, a maternal-looking Asian woman named Mrs. Kennedy, glanced up. "Hello, Carole," she said sympathetically. "Dr. Durbin is waiting for you. Go right in."

Carole nodded her thanks, not trusting her voice to speak. Then she turned and stepped past the reception desk and down a short, brightly lit hallway. Several doors opened off the hall, and most of them were open—Carole could see the principal, Mr. Price, and the two guidance counselors sitting at their desks, talking on the phone or doing paperwork. But the vice principal's door was shut. Carole hesitantly raised her fist and knocked softly.

"Come in!" the response came at once, short and sharp.

Carole pushed open the door and stepped inside. The vice principal glanced up, nodded, and gestured at one of the hard wooden chairs facing the spotless metal desk. "Have a seat."

Carole crept forward and perched on the edge of the chair. She arranged her hands on her lap and glanced around quickly, curious in spite of herself. She had never been inside this office before, but she had heard horror stories from other students who had visited it. They mostly made it sound like a combination of a medieval dungeon and the manure pit at Pine Hollow. But in reality, it looked like a normal school office—nothing more, nothing less. Dusty venetian blinds blocked the bright Virginia sunlight from the two narrow windows. Several framed family photos hung on the beige-painted walls. A large potted plant sat in one corner. Nothing scary at all.

The vice principal herself was another matter. Dr. Durbin was a brisk, businesslike woman in her early fifties, with salt-and-pepper hair and piercing green eyes that had the ability to cut right through people. Carole had heard of more than one tough customer who'd dissolved into a puddle of helpless goo in the face of that steely gaze. Bracing herself, she cautiously peeked across the desk at the vice principal.

"Carole Hanson," Dr. Durbin said deliberately, glancing at her calendar. "Carole Hanson. I don't think I've seen you in my office before, have I, Ms. Hanson?"

"N-No," Carole squeaked. She cleared her throat, willing herself to sound a little less pathetic. "I mean, no, ma'am. I've never been here before."

Dr. Durbin nodded and leaned back in her chair, tapping her fountain pen against the edge of the desk and studying Carole's face carefully. "Well now," she said at last, so suddenly that

Carole jumped in her chair. "Why don't you fill me in on this cheating business?"

Carole swallowed hard, wondering how much Ms. Shepard had told the vice principal. "Well . . . ," she began tentatively. "Um, I didn't really mean to do it, but I—"

"Didn't mean to?" Dr. Durbin broke in sharply. "What happened, did your textbook jump out of your bag by itself? Did someone hold your eyes open and force you to look at those answers?"

Carole winced, feeling as though she'd been slapped. But she knew that Dr. Durbin was only calling her on her own self-deception. "No," she said weakly. "I did it. I know it was wrong. Even while I was doing it I realized it. But I felt like I had to, because I didn't want to flunk the semester. But I know that's no excuse—I should have studied more. I'm sorry."

Dr. Durbin nodded, seeming somewhat satisfied by that. "Well now," she said. "Remorse. That's what I like to hear. So what are we going to do about this, Ms. Hanson?"

Carole wasn't sure whether it was a rhetorical question or not. She decided to play it safe and answer. "Ms. Shepard assigned me a research paper," she offered. "To make up the material on, um, that test."

"Yes." Dr. Durbin nodded and pursed her

lips, still gazing at Carole intently, like a scientist studying a bug on the end of a pin. "A research paper. Very good. But you must know that I can't simply look the other way in a case like this. I'm going to have to add an official punishment from the school."

That was the sentence Carole had been dreading. "Um, I understand," she said in a voice that was little more than a whisper. This was it—the moment when she would learn her fate. Suspension? Expulsion? A year's worth of detention?

Dr. Durbin leaned forward and rested her elbows on her desk, still gazing at Carole. But now her expression was thoughtful. "Carole Hanson," she said deliberately. "Carole, it would be a real shame to suspend you over this, since it is your first offense, serious or otherwise."

Carole kept silent, holding her breath. She knew that Stevie would have come up with some kind of funny response to lighten the tension, something like *Yes, I agree, that would definitely be a shame.* And Lisa might say something responsible and supportive, like *I appreciate your saying that.*

But Carole couldn't say a word. All she could do was wait to see where Dr. Durbin was going with this. She twisted her hands in her lap, trying to prepare herself for the worst.

"I think I may have a better idea, though,"

the vice principal went on. "Carole, have you ever heard of an organization called Hometown Hope?"

Carole blinked, a little startled by the sudden change of topic. "Er, yes," she said. "It's a volunteer group that fixes up abandoned buildings and stuff in this part of the county. My dad spoke at a benefit dinner for them a couple of months ago."

"Hanson!" Dr. Durbin's face lit up, and she smacked herself on the forehead. "Of course! I thought your name sounded familiar. Mitch Hanson is your father?"

Carole nodded, still feeling perplexed by the shift of direction. Was Dr. Durbin ever going to tell her what her punishment would be?

Dr. Durbin didn't keep her in suspense for too long. "Well now, then you may also know that Hometown Hope is based right here in Willow Creek. But judging by the confused look on your face right now, I'll bet you don't know that I'm the volunteer coordinator for the group."

Carole shook her head. "No," she said. "I had no idea."

"I suppose that means you don't find our morning announcements very enthralling," Dr. Durbin said with the ghost of a smile. "Because I spoke about the group just last week, asking the students here to consider donating their time to our next project."

Carole blushed and shifted her weight on her chair. "Um, I guess I don't always listen to those as carefully as I should," she admitted, thinking about all the times she'd sat daydreaming in homeroom, coming back to reality only when the first bell broke into her thoughts of Samson or Starlight or other Pine Hollow–related subjects.

"Well, perhaps you might think about paying more attention in the future," Dr. Durbin said, not unkindly. "In the meantime, what would you say to doing a little community service in lieu of suspension or detention?"

"You mean working for Hometown Hope?" Carole was finally catching on.

The vice principal nodded, leaning back in her chair again. "We have a new project coming up, refurbishing a run-down park over on the other side of Whitby Street," she said. "It's pretty easy to get volunteers for outdoor work when the weather's nice. But in November, well . . ." She spread out her hands expressively. "We're a little short on able-bodied help. Especially since we plan to get started this weekend and work right through Thanksgiving week if we have to. So what do you say?"

Carole wanted to make sure she understood.

"You mean if I volunteer for Hometown Hope, I won't get suspended?"

Dr. Durbin chuckled. "That's what I'm saying," she agreed. "Do we have a deal?"

Carole almost grinned. She wasn't going to be suspended! She wouldn't even have to serve detention. Besides that, volunteering for Hometown Hope was probably the only way she was going to escape from her house for the next six weeks. And throwing herself into some hard physical labor definitely sounded better at the moment than sitting around in her bedroom all alone, brooding over all the fun she was missing at Pine Hollow and maybe doing a few pathetic sit-ups and leg lifts to try to keep her riding muscles in shape.

"We have a deal," she told Dr. Durbin quickly. "Um, I'll just have to check with my dad first. I'm supposed to be grounded, and well . . ."

Dr. Durbin nodded. "Fine," she said. "Would it help if I called him myself and explained our deal to him?"

"Probably," Carole answered. "If you want to call him this afternoon, he should be home right after lunch." She hesitated. "So if he says yes, what do I need to do? I mean, to get started."

Dr. Durbin rubbed her hands together and leaned forward again, looking eager. "There's a planning meeting Wednesday afternoon," she said. "It's at the community center over in that new development, Willow Woods. Do you know where that is?"

Carole shook her head. "Sorry."

"No problem. You can follow me over there after school." Dr. Durbin smiled. "All right, then, you'd better get back to lunch and finish eating. You're going to need all the energy you can get once we put you to work!"

"Phil?" Stevie said into the phone, leaning back against the kitchen counter. "Hi, it's me."

"Hi, me," Phil replied. "What's up?"

"Did you talk to him?"

"I did," Phil replied. "We're all set for Wednesday afternoon. A.J. actually seemed kind of psyched about it."

"Really?" Stevie felt a twinge of hope. If A.J. was excited about hanging out with her and Phil, maybe that meant he was coming back to his senses. Maybe he was over his attitude problems and ready to talk to his friends again. If so, maybe they would finally be able to help him. "That's great. I'm psyched, too."

"I'm psyched that I'll get to see you," Phil replied. "Even if I have to share you with A.J. So we'll meet at Cross County right after school, okay? Then it'll be off into the wilderness, just the three of us. See you then."

"Bye." Stevie felt a slight pang as she hung up the phone. It would have been nice if it had been just the *two* of them. It had been a long while since she'd spent any quality time alone with Phil, so long that she had almost forgotten what it was like. But she did her best to push such selfish thoughts out of her mind. A.J. needed them right now, and that was the most important thing.

Phil and I will have plenty of time to hang out when I'm ungrounded, she told herself. *And if A.J. keeps on the way he's been going, who knows how much time we have to get through to him?*

6

SIX

As her classmates jogged over to take their places on either side of the volleyball net in the Fenton Hall gym, Callie took her usual seat on the lowest row of bleachers. Because of her bad leg, she was excused from participating in phys ed for the entire semester. But that didn't mean she was excused from attending. Twice a week since the beginning of the school year, she had been forced to sit there for the whole class period, watching her classmates run laps or practice their tennis swings or do sit-ups. Or play volleyball, as they were doing today.

What a waste, Callie thought with a sigh, not for the first time. Pushing her blond hair out of her face, she idly watched as Ms. Monroe called the class to order. *I wonder what kind of educational experience this is supposed to be.*

She couldn't help smiling at the thought. Before being elected to the House of Representatives in the last election, her father had been a state representative. One of his duties had been chairing a committee on improving the public school system, and during that time the talk around the family dinner table had focused an awful lot on things like "educational experiences."

Callie's smile faded. Thinking about those days reminded her of her life back in Valley Vista, which brought her back to a topic that was never far from her mind this week—her family's upcoming trip.

Okay, so maybe I can't play volleyball, she thought. *That doesn't mean I have to just sit here and veg out. This doesn't have to be a total waste of time.*

Shooting a quick look at the volleyball game, which was in full swing, Callie was just in time to see Stevie dive for a wild ball. Veronica di-Angelo, who was busy examining her fingernails, took a casual step in the wrong direction and almost collided with her. Stevie threw herself aside just in time, landing hard on one knee as the ball bounced away toward the locker rooms.

"Watch it!" Stevie cried in frustration, rubbing her knee and glaring at Veronica as she climbed to her feet. "If you're not going to play, at least stay out of my way!"

Veronica just shrugged, not even bothering to look up from her stylish French manicure.

"Don't blame me, Stevie," she said calmly. "It's your own fault if you're a spaz, not mine."

Callie shook her head, wondering how her brother could ever have seen anything in Veronica. For a while there, it had seemed that the two of them were really becoming an item. During Scott's campaign for student body president, Veronica had been all but glued to his side, talking him up to her legion of friends and admirers, laughing at his every witty remark, and generally acting the part of adoring groupie. Then Scott had told her he just wanted to be friends. That clearly wasn't something Veronica had wanted to hear, and she hadn't let him forget it since. She really had it in for him, and that meant she wasn't exactly looking to be best friends with Callie, either.

It's Scott's own fault, Callie thought idly as she watched Veronica whisper something to her friend Nicole, who giggled and shot Stevie a quick glance. Stevie ignored them both, focusing on the ball as a teammate served it cleanly over the net. *If he wasn't such a flirt, he wouldn't have this kind of problem.* It wasn't the first time she'd thought along those lines, and she didn't waste much time on it. She knew her brother could take care of himself.

Instead she returned her attention to her own situation. Pushing her books and her crutches out of the way, she planted both hands on the bleacher seat and then concentrated on her weak leg. Her therapeutic riding sessions had helped a lot to strengthen and recondition her muscles, but her doctor had assigned her some additional exercises, which she had been doing faithfully every morning and evening in her bedroom. Concentrating on keeping the correct position, she slowly lifted her leg six inches off the floor, held it for a count of three, then lowered it just as slowly. One rep. Then another. Then another.

When her thigh muscles started to ache, she switched to a second exercise that worked a different set of muscles. She did twice her usual number of reps before returning to the first exercise. By the second set her weary limb started to protest and her leg shook slightly as she lifted it again and again.

Come on, come on, she chided herself, gritting her teeth as beads of sweat broke out on her forehead and upper lip. *You can do this. You know you can.*

She was focusing so hard on controlling her muscles, on making them do what she wanted, that she barely heard the phys ed teacher call for a time-out. Callie was unaware that several of her classmates had turned to stare at her until she heard a sardonic voice mention her name loudly.

"Check it out, everyone!" Veronica exclaimed

with barely concealed sarcasm. "I think Callie's having some kind of seizure. Should I call nine-one-one?"

Callie looked up quickly, letting her foot fall back to the floor with a bang. She winced at the impact, which jarred her joints clear to her hipbone.

But before she could come up with a suitable comeback, Stevie spoke up. "Shove it, Veronica," she said. "It figures *you* wouldn't recognize actual exercise when you saw it."

Veronica rolled her eyes. "That's rich, coming from someone who spends a whole lot more time exercising her mouth than her body."

"Oh yeah?" Stevie replied more hotly than ever. "Well, maybe polishing your fingernails seems like exercise to a witch like you, but—"

"Stephanie Lake!" Ms. Monroe interrupted sharply. "I will not have that sort of talk in my class! Do I make myself clear, or do you want to go and discuss it with Miss Fenton?"

Veronica tossed her sleek, dark hair over her shoulder. "Thank you for your support, Ms. Monroe." She turned and glared at Stevie icily before returning her attention to the teacher. "But you probably shouldn't waste Miss Fenton's time. It's not as though I care what some-one like her thinks of me." She tilted her head dismissively in Stevie's general direction.

Ms. Monroe looked uncertain how to respond to that. Finally she shrugged and clapped her hands briskly. "Just watch yourself, Lake. All right, people," she barked. "Back in position. Move!"

Callie saw Stevie shooting her a concerned glance, but she didn't meet her eye. She knew that Stevie meant well, but she couldn't help feeling embarrassed and a little resentful. She wasn't used to needing other people to defend her—she could handle a jerk like Veronica, bum leg or no. And it irked her that anyone might think otherwise.

She glanced at her crutches. *I've got to lose these stupid things before we leave for Valley Vista this weekend,* she thought with determination. *No matter what it takes!*

Carole was surprised to find the library already crowded when she arrived there soon after the final bell. Students were seated at most of the blond-wood-and-steel tables that dotted the spacious reading area in the central atrium, and others were searching for books in the rows of stacks surrounding the atrium. Carole blinked. *Wow,* she thought. *So this is what other people do after school.*

She sighed, wishing she were on her way to Pine Hollow as usual instead of standing in the library entrance facing a dull afternoon of studying. Even hosing down the manure pit or helping the beginning riders find their boots in their messy cubbyholes would be a treat compared to what she had to do. Hoisting her backpack higher on her shoulder, she wandered past the librarians' desk and through the atrium, looking for a seat. Halfway to the back of the room, she spotted a free space.

Joy Harper, a girl Carole knew slightly from a few of her classes, was sitting across from the empty spot, her books, jacket, and papers spilling across the table. "Is this seat taken?" Carole asked her.

Joy glanced up from her math book and shook her head, pushing back her thick dark bangs. "Nope. It's all yours." She leaned forward and scooped her things toward her, making room for Carole.

"Thanks." Carole set her backpack on the table and pulled out the chair. Collapsing into it, she just sat there for a moment, wondering where to start. She had combed her textbook the evening before, hoping for inspiration. But she had been too distracted by the mere act of surviving her first day without Pine Hollow to come up with anything decent. She regretted the wasted time now, though, knowing that she had to find a topic for her research paper by the next day, or Ms. Shepard just might rethink her decision not to flunk her.

How did I get myself into this mess, anyway? Carole thought miserably, unzipping her backpack and pulling out her American history book. She grimaced as a little voice in her head piped up with the answer: *You did something really stupid, that's how.*

At least she could stop worrying about being suspended, thanks to Dr. Durbin's volunteer group. Colonel Hanson had been gung ho about the vice principal's proposal. He had quickly given his permission for Carole to attend Wednesday's meeting and to put in as many hours as she liked with the group as long as she kept up with her homework.

She opened her textbook, blinking at the table of contents. Flipping to a likely chapter, she settled down to read. But she was only a few sentences in when her attention started to wander. She found herself wondering whether she'd remembered to replace the antiseptic she'd borrowed the week before from the stable first-aid kit. That reminded her that she hadn't looked in on Congo after the horse show to make sure that the small scrape on his hock was healing properly. Then there was Peso, one of the ponies— had she remembered to tell Max about that funny bump on his hoof?

It wasn't easy to push those sorts of questions out of her mind, but Carole did her best, reminding herself that Max was more than capable of running the stable without her. After all, he'd done it for years before she'd ever heard of the place. . . .

Carole started the history chapter again, blinking hard several times and doing her best to focus on the words in front of her. But once again, it wasn't long before the description of nineteenth century immigration practices faded, to be replaced by images of Samson languishing in his stall with no one to exercise him properly, and of Red and Denise and the others rushing around with extra work to finish, thanks to her absence.

This wasn't going to be easy. *How am I supposed to concentrate on this stuff?* Carole wondered helplessly. *How am I supposed to figure out whether I'd rather write about immigration or Prohibition or the early days of suffrage when all I can think about is everything I'm missing right this minute at Pine Hollow?*

She sighed and rubbed her eyes, hoping she could rub away the images that kept dancing through her mind. Samson tossing his head and gazing at her with his fiery dark eyes. Starlight trotting around the schooling ring with Rachel in his saddle. Max looking at her with disap-

81

pointment and surprise in his blue eyes as she told him what she'd done. And Ben . . .

When she looked up again, Carole noticed that Adam Levine had just entered the library and was heading toward her table. Back in junior high Adam had taken lessons at Pine Hollow for a while. He had long since dropped riding in favor of working on his junked-out old Mustang, but his appearance still reminded Carole of old times—like the way Adam always tilted his toes out a little too much when he cantered around the ring on Barq or Rusty or Tecumseh, or the way Max used to yell at Betsy Cavanaugh for flirting with Adam during riding class, or the fun times they'd all had together, the whole class, at gymkhanas and schooling shows and the yearly overnight summer trail ride . . .

Lost in the past, Carole smiled uncertainly at Adam as he loped toward her table. For one crazy moment, she was sure he was there to talk to her about riding—maybe get her opinion on a new pair of boots or ask if she would help him with his lead changes. . . .

Then she blushed as she remembered that Adam was dating Joy, who was still sitting right across from her. Carole generally didn't pay much attention to the shifting romantic lives of her classmates, but Adam and Joy were both in her English class, and Carole had seen them often enough passing notes and blowing kisses when the teacher's back was turned. Now, as she watched, Adam crept toward Joy, whose back was toward him. Catching Carole looking at him, Adam grinned and winked at her, putting one finger to his lips in a gesture of silence.

When he was just inches away, he leaped forward, clapping his hands over Joy's eyes. "Surprise!" he whispered.

Joy squealed, bringing glances from most of the students in the atrium and a stern look from the nearest librarian. But she ignored them all, grabbing Adam's hands and spinning to face him. "You monster!" she exclaimed fondly. "You scared the spit out of me!"

"Sorry, I couldn't resist," Adam replied with a grin. "Don't hold it against me, okay?"

"It's okay, sweetie," Joy said, batting her eyelashes playfully. "How could I possibly stay mad at someone so cute?"

Adam's grin broadened. "I don't know," he said. "How could you?"

Carole averted her eyes as the couple laughed together and then shared an affectionate kiss, seemingly unaware that they had an audience. Carole knew how they felt, at least sort of. When Ben had kissed her the other day, she had ceased to be aware of anything else—even her pain at losing Samson, her job, and just about everything else had receded as she had lost herself in the feeling of being so close to him, of finally feeling as though they might begin to understand each other completely.

I wish I'd found a minute to tell Stevie and Lisa about that, Carole thought, feeling her cheeks grow hot as she remembered that kiss. *I could use their advice. Maybe they could tell me how I'm supposed to face Ben if and when I'm ever allowed back to Pine Hollow.*

Carole sometimes felt a bit awkward about being the only one of their trio who had never had a serious boyfriend. The closest she had ever come was way back in junior high, when she'd gone out for a while with a guy from a nearby town named Cam Nelson. But Cam's family had moved away before that could turn into anything serious, and somehow Carole hadn't been interested in anyone since then.

Then Ben had come along. Carole still wasn't sure what she was expecting to happen after their kiss. But it wasn't to have him look straight through her as if he wished they'd never met. It definitely wasn't that at all.

Glancing down at her textbook, Carole realized that it was hopeless to try to come up with a topic right then. She was in no state to concentrate on schoolwork. Not when she was feeling so sad and hopeless and distracted and, worst of all, alone. She couldn't talk to her father about her feelings—not when he was still so angry with her. She wasn't allowed to use the phone, send e-mail, or leave the house without permission, so that left out her friends. Even her usual source of comfort and solace in times of trouble, Pine Hollow, was forbidden to her. All she had was herself.

Leaving her backpack on the table, she stood up quickly and headed into the stacks, needing to be alone before she totally lost it. She checked each aisle, but the library was more crowded than before, and people stood in almost every one. Heading farther toward the back, Carole felt a sharp stab of recognition as she stumbled across the section that held the library's small collection of horse-related materials. Once upon a time she had spent many hours there, though by now she'd all but memorized every book on the shelf. Remembering the way she'd once looked up information on foxhunting and researched flying lead changes when Starlight was having trouble with them made her heart ache all the more. As she turned away from the painfully familiar titles on the shelves, she felt tears stinging her eyes.

Finally, near the rear of the library, she found a deserted aisle. There was nothing on the tall, narrow metal shelves back there but a few boxes of old magazines and some stray books waiting to be shelved, so she wasn't likely to be interrupted anytime soon.

Sinking to the carpeted floor, she dropped her face onto her arms and let the tears come.

In Mary Shelley's great novel Frankenstein, *the character of the monster is distinct in his solitude from all humanity,* Lisa typed. *He was created from Man and by Man, yet he stands apart from those around him, including his creator. He is all alone.*

She sat back and gazed at the computer screen, rereading the sentences. Then she sighed.

Just like me, she typed. *All alone without Prancer.*

She scowled and hit the Delete button to erase the last part of what she'd written. It wouldn't do any good to sit there and feel sorry for herself. That wouldn't bring Prancer back, and it certainly wouldn't help her pass her advanced senior lit class.

With a frustrated groan, Lisa picked up her paperback copy of *Frankenstein* and leafed through it, trying to find her train of thought. But other thoughts kept intruding. Sad thoughts of Prancer. The unpleasant memory of Rafe walking into her kitchen yesterday as if he owned it. Of Mrs. Atwood's latest lecture about what

86

she'd referred to as "this whole college fiasco," delivered over breakfast that morning.

The phone rang, and Lisa jumped up and hurried out into the hall to answer it, relieved at the interruption. "Hello?" she said.

"Lisa? Hey, it's me," Alex's familiar voice came over the line. "What's up?"

Lisa smiled and felt herself relax just a bit. "Nothing much." She leaned against the hall's muted floral wallpaper and switched the phone to her other ear. "Mom's at work, so I was taking advantage of the peace and quiet by doing some homework. What about you? Aren't you supposed to be grounded?" She didn't want to be a nag, but she really hoped he wasn't breaking his punishment to call her. If he was, his parents might take back their permission for the next afternoon's date. And if Lisa didn't have that to look forward to, she wasn't sure what she would do.

"I can only talk for a second," Alex admitted. "I told Mom I needed to call you to confirm our plans for tomorrow. So are we still on?"

"No doubt about it," Lisa replied quickly. "Where should we meet?"

"I'll walk over when I get home from school," Alex replied. "Stevie needs the car tomorrow, so I was hoping you could drive."

"No problem. So are you sure you don't mind

going to that exhibit? I know modern sculpture isn't really your thing."

"Ah, but zat eez where you are wrong, mademoiselle," Alex retorted in his best imitation of a snooty French accent. "I am ze expert on all ze finest of ze fine arz."

Lisa giggled. Alex had always been a lot more interested in Michael Jordan than Monet, and they both knew it. Normally she had to drag him, kicking and screaming, to any event that he suspected might be the least bit cultural. She was sure that Prancer had something to do with his new attitude, though the fact that they hadn't been on a real date in ages probably had an impact, too. She knew exactly how he felt on that point. If he'd been dying to go to some kind of bloody kick boxing match on Wednesday afternoon, she would have gladly gone along with the plan just for the chance to spend time with him.

"Okay, then," she said. "Don't say I didn't give you a chance to back out. What time do you have to be home? Maybe we could get something to eat afterward."

"Definitely," Alex agreed. "I don't have to be home until six-thirty or so. Plus I was hoping you'd help me pick out a new pair of basketball sneakers. The season starts soon, you know, and the coach practically promised I'd make varsity this year, so I want to be ready."

"Okay." Lisa smiled as she remembered watching some of Alex's JV basketball games the previous winter. He looked awfully cute in Fenton Hall's crimson-and-gold uniform. "It's a date."

"Spiffy," Alex said. "Okay, then, I'd better cruise. I'll see you tomorrow. I love you."

"Me too. See you then." Lisa hung up the phone and wandered back into her room. She had just taken her seat in front of the computer when the phone rang again. With a fond smile, she hurried out to pick it up. "What did you forget?" she asked teasingly.

"Lisa?" A voice came through the line, deeper and more mature than Alex's reedy tenor.

"Oops. Um, hi, Dad," Lisa said. "Sorry, I thought you were someone else."

"Hmm," Mr. Atwood said. "Well, I'm just calling to confirm the schedule for this weekend. Don't forget, you have to be at the airport a little early on Saturday to pick up your boarding pass."

"I know," Lisa replied, rubbing a smudge of dirt off the phone cradle. "Mom already switched her schedule so she can drive me."

"Er, yes." Her father sounded a little uncomfortable, as he usually did when the subject of his ex-wife cropped up in conversation. "All right, then, Evelyn and I will pick you up on this end.

Maybe we can swing past USC on our way home."

"Dad . . . ," Lisa began helplessly. Her father had made it perfectly clear in previous phone conversations that he disapproved of her plan to go to NVU as thoroughly as Lisa's mother did.

"Don't 'Dad' me, Lisa," he said. "This is a very important life decision of yours that we're talking about. I want to make sure you understand what you're doing before it's too late. It won't do you any harm to check out some of your other options more carefully."

Lisa wanted to argue that she'd already made up her mind and any further discussion was a big waste of time, but she didn't have the energy. "Fine," she said instead. "I hear they have some cool coffee shops near there. At least I'll be able to fight jet lag."

"Lisa," Mr. Atwood began sternly. "This really isn't—"

"Kidding, Dad," Lisa interrupted hastily. "I'm just kidding."

"All right." He didn't sound convinced. "But we're going to have a good long talk about this decision when you get here—and I'm not kidding about that. Do you hear me?"

"Uh-huh." Lisa grimaced, feeling her stomach twist into a familiar knot of anxiety. Why couldn't her parents just accept that she'd made this decision on her own? She would be eighteen in a few short months—a legal adult. It was about time she took control of her own life. "Listen, I need to get back to my homework," she told her father. "I'll see you on Saturday, okay?"

Mr. Atwood said good-bye, and Lisa hung up the phone with a sigh, wondering if spending the next week in California listening to her father lecture her about college would be more or less pleasant than spending it in Willow Creek watching her mother and Rafe carry on and thinking about how much she missed Prancer. It was pretty much a toss-up, which depressed her more than ever.

At least I have one thing to look forward to, she told herself, thinking of the next day's date. *If I didn't have Alex right now, I don't know what I'd do.*

SEVEN

"Carole!" a voice called breathlessly. "Carole, wait up! I just heard the news."

Carole paused on her way through the school's glass double doors. She was on her way to the student parking lot to pick up her car, and she was in a hurry—Dr. Durbin was waiting for her in the teachers' parking lot so that Carole could follow her to the Hometown Hope meeting. Glancing around impatiently, Carole saw Polly Giacomin hurrying to catch up. Polly was a senior at Willow Creek High School and the owner of a spunky brown gelding named Romeo that had been a boarder at Pine Hollow for the past several years. Despite that, Carole had never felt particularly close to Polly. Polly always seemed to be speaking a slightly different language—one that sounded the same as Carole's but didn't quite connect in her head.

"Hi," Carole greeted her tentatively. Carole and Polly never had much to say to each other except when discussing their horses' latest antics, and at the moment Carole wasn't exactly in the mood for a nice chat about Romeo's progress in dressage.

Polly reached her side. "I just heard," she repeated. "You must be so bummed! I mean, what a total surprise. To everyone."

Carole winced, assuming that Polly was referring to the loss of her job at the stable. "Yeah," she said. "I figured everybody must have found out about that by now."

But it turned out that Polly had something else on her mind. "What do you mean?" she asked. "Oh, did you know that Max was talking to that Canadian guy about Samson?"

"Samson?" Carole felt confused. "Wait a minute. What are you talking about?"

"About Samson leaving," Polly said. "I just ran into Andrea, and she said Max told her he's shipping Samson up to Canada this afternoon. I mean, I knew he was going, but I didn't realize it would be so fast."

Carole's head spun. Some tiny rational part of her brain knew that she shouldn't be surprised—naturally Samson's new owner was eager to have him as soon as possible. And Max had no reason to hold him at Pine Hollow. But that didn't lessen the shock of Polly's words. "T-Today?" Carole stammered. "Are you sure?"

Polly shrugged. "That's what Andrea told me. I guess you could check with Max if—oops, sorry. Maybe not." She looked embarrassed. "I, uh, I heard about—well, you know. Sorry."

Carole hardly heard her. Mumbling something about being late, she walked off toward the parking lot without a backward glance. She felt numb all over. Somehow, she managed to find her way to her small, rust-red car and climb inside. Moving on autopilot, she got the keys out of her pocket and into the ignition. She started to turn toward the exit, remembering only at the last moment that she needed to go the other way, to the teachers' parking lot.

When she pulled into the teachers' lot, she immediately spotted Dr. Durbin standing beside a biscuit-colored sedan that looked as businesslike and no-nonsense as she did herself. "Ready to go, Carole?" the vice principal called cheerfully as Carole pulled up next to her.

Carole pasted a weak smile on her face as she idled behind Dr. Durbin's car. "I'm ready," she lied. "I'll follow you."

Dr. Durbin was an unhurried driver, and Carole had no trouble keeping up as she drove across town, heading in the opposite direction from Carole's house. Leaving the town limits, the vice principal led the way through several housing developments before turning in at a rustic-looking wooden sign reading WILLOW WOODS. Before long Carole was parking her car beside the vice principal's in the small parking lot in front of an unassuming frame building.

"Here we are," Dr. Durbin called as Carole climbed out of her car. "Right on time."

"Uh-huh." Carole was still thinking about Samson. She couldn't believe he was leaving that very day. She would never see him again, except maybe on TV when he competed with his new owner in Grand Prix events.

She followed Dr. Durbin into the building, which consisted primarily of a large meeting room with folding metal chairs set up facing a podium. A dozen people were already inside, seated on the chairs or standing near the podium chatting. A few of them noticed Dr. Durbin's entrance and waved a greeting. One earnest-looking young man with receding sandy brown hair detached himself from a small group and hurried toward the newcomers.

"Jan," he called. "Good, you're here. Should we get started?"

"In a second," Dr. Durbin said. "First I'd like you to meet our newest volunteer. Carole Hanson, this is Craig Skippack, our fearless leader."

"Nice to meet you," Carole said automatically. Craig replied politely, welcoming her to the meeting, but Carole didn't really hear his words. She was picturing Samson paused at the foot of a loading ramp, sniffing it carefully as if checking to make sure it was solid.

I can't believe I won't be there to say good-bye to him, she thought dully, following Dr. Durbin toward a row of chairs and taking a seat. *I thought I was ready for this, but I didn't think it would happen so soon. . . .*

More memories flooded her mind. Samson being born—balancing on his long, slender legs for the first time, looking around in wonder at the new world surrounding him. The first time Max put a halter on the gangly, energetic, curious foal. That day, Samson had bucked and kicked and shaken his head from side to side as if he might never stop, though he'd calmed down within a few days. Then there was the first time the spirited young horse had competed in a real show. Lisa had ridden him that day, and the gelding's talent had been evident even though he was still green. And then there were the past few months—a time Carole had thought would last forever, their time together. From the first day the black horse had returned to Pine Hollow, Carole had spent most of her waking moments thinking of him, training him, riding him. It had all paid off on Saturday at the show, when they had qualified for the jump-off against the toughest possible competition. And when they had triumphed, when the judge had pinned the blue ribbon to Samson's bridle and the horse had snorted as if he understood what they had done—

"Carole!" Dr. Durbin whispered sharply.

Blinking and sitting up quickly, Carole realized that she had become completely lost in her trip down Memory Lane. Craig Skippack was at the podium saying something about playground equipment and indoor-outdoor paint. Most of the others in the room were listening raptly, but Dr. Durbin was glaring at Carole, the annoyance clear in her eyes.

"Are you with us, Carole?" the vice principal whispered.

Carole gulped. "Sorry," she murmured. "I—I guess I'm a little distracted today."

"If you'd prefer, we could revisit the suspension idea," Dr. Durbin whispered sternly. "If you're not going to take this seriously, then I really think—"

"No, no," Carole whispered back hastily. "I'm sorry, really. I want to do this. It's just that, um . . ." She searched her mind for a feasible excuse. Somehow she didn't think that the truth would impress the vice principal very much. "Uh, I'm not feeling too well," she blurted out. "I have a stomachache."

Dr. Durbin looked skeptical for a moment.

But apparently the real pain in Carole's eyes convinced her that she was telling the truth. "Well now," she said at last. "If that's the case, maybe you ought to get home to bed. I can fill you in tomorrow, or I can have Craig call you with the details."

Carole could hardly believe her ears. "Uh, okay," she said, pretending to be reluctant. "Maybe that would be best. I'm sorry." Clutching her stomach for effect, she carefully slid out of her seat and headed for the door.

Outside, she broke into a run. She had no intention of going home to bed. There was only one place in the world that she wanted to be right then, and she was going to have to hurry.

Phil was leading his bay gelding, Teddy, up the hard-packed dirt driveway of Cross County Stables when Stevie took the turn off the country highway. Pulling up slowly beside them as Phil guided the athletic quarter horse to one side of the drive, she rolled down her window.

"Yo!" she called. "Get that beast off the road. I'm trying to drive here!"

Phil grinned. "You'd better watch it, or I'll ask Mr. Baker to put you on Bunny today," he joked.

Stevie returned his grin. Bunny was a large, ornery one-eyed mule that hated every living creature with a passion, except for his stablemate, a boarder's Thoroughbred gelding. "So where's A.J.?" Stevie asked Phil. "Isn't he with you?"

"He's already here, I think," Phil reported. "I saw him ride past my house on his bike a few minutes ago, heading this way."

Stevie nodded. As nice as it would have been to have Phil all to herself, she was glad to hear that A.J. hadn't bailed on them. She was determined not to give up on him, even if it sometimes seemed that he'd given up on himself. "Good. Meet you up there," she told Phil before tapping the gas pedal and pulling ahead, turning off on the side road that led to the small parking lot.

A few minutes later Teddy was tied to the wooden hitching post outside the front door and Stevie and Phil were walking into the stable building arm in arm. Cross County Stables was smaller and slightly more rustic in appearance than Pine Hollow, but it was just as clean, efficient, and well run, thanks to Mr. Baker, the manager and a close friend of Max's. Stevie had been a regular visitor there since she and Phil had met back in junior high.

"Who am I riding today?" she asked Phil as they walked down the long narrow main stable aisle. Unlike Pine Hollow with its U-shaped aisle, which was flanked on both sides by stalls,

Cross County's L-shaped main aisle had stalls on only one side. The other side was lined with windows that looked out onto the stable's central courtyard, which held a mounting block and a small riding ring.

"Well, I suggested Teeny," Phil said, referring to a hulking retired Percheron. Teeny spent most of his time grazing in one of the stable's hilly back pastures. "But Mr. Baker seemed to think Blue was a better choice."

"Cool." Stevie was happy to hear that one of her favorite Cross County horses was available. Blue was no Belle—she didn't have Belle's mischievous spirit or her talent for dressage—but she was a good horse in her own quieter, more serious way. Stevie had ridden the easygoing dark gray mare during many previous visits to Cross County.

Blue's stall was near the end of the row. On the way there, Stevie paused in front of the stall housing A.J.'s horse, a gray mare named Crystal. "He's not in there," she reported, patting Crystal on the nose and peering past her into the stall.

"He's probably in the tack room," Phil said. "I'll go check on him."

"Bring Blue's tack while you're at it, okay?" Stevie said. "I'm going to go say hello and get reacquainted."

"Be right back." Phil hurried off down the

aisle. After one last pat for Crystal, Stevie headed in the other direction and soon reached Blue's stall.

"How's it going, girlfriend?" Stevie greeted the horse cheerfully, unhooking the webbing from the front of the stall. Blue came forward with a snort, tossing her long mane and sniffing the top of Stevie's head curiously.

Stevie giggled and wrinkled her nose. Less than a minute later, Phil turned up in the stall door carrying a saddle and bridle. "A.J.'s there," he reported. "Turns out Mr. Baker noticed he hadn't cleaned his tack the last time out. I interrupted the lecture."

"I guess he takes that stuff just as seriously as Max does," Stevie commented, remembering the many lectures Max had given her about keeping her tack spick-and-span. "Toss me that bridle, will you?"

Phil handed over the bridle agreeably. "I'll meet you out front, okay?" he said. "I'm going to go hurry A.J. along, and then I'd better check on Teddy."

"See you in a few." Giving Blue a fond pat on the neck, Stevie set about tacking up the mare, chatting to her easily the whole time.

Inside, though, Stevie was feeling a nervous twinge in the pit of her stomach about their upcoming ride. She wasn't sure why this attempt to get through to A.J. should seem any more important than their many previous tries. But it did. She couldn't shake the feeling that it could be their last chance. Maybe it was all the stories she'd been hearing about A.J.'s drinking. Maybe it was that Thanksgiving was approaching rapidly, the mother of all family holidays, and A.J. was still estranged from his own family. Maybe it was simply that the situation had been going on far too long. Stevie wasn't sure. But she knew she was going to do whatever it took to help her friend get past all his problems.

A few minutes later, as Stevie was slipping the girth beneath Blue's smooth, slightly rounded belly, she heard the sound of laughter just down the aisle. Familiar laughter. "Sounds like A.J.'s in a good mood," she murmured into the mare's warm side. Quickly pulling the girth snug and fastening it securely, Stevie gave the horse a pat and stepped to the front of the stall.

A.J. and Phil were just a few yards away in front of Crystal's stall. A.J. was holding his horse's saddle and grinning at whatever Phil was saying to him—Stevie was too far away to hear.

Seeing Stevie watching them, Phil waved. "Almost ready?" he called.

"Almost," she replied. Ducking back into the stall, she quickly finished getting Blue ready. Then she led the mare out into the aisle, just in time to follow Crystal as A.J. led her toward the door.

"This was a great idea, Stevie," A.J. said as Stevie led Blue to the mounting block and swung herself aboard. "And don't worry, I brought enough cookies for everyone." He patted the backpack he was holding. "Nothing like a balanced meal, right?"

"Oops!" Stevie realized that she'd forgotten about the sandwiches she'd packed for the three of them. "The food! It's still in the car."

She made a move to dismount, but Phil held up his hand. "Stay put," he ordered. "I'll go get it."

Stevie grinned gratefully. "My hero."

Phil rolled his eyes and tossed her Teddy's reins. Then he took off for the parking lot at a jog.

Stevie turned to look at A.J. This could be her only chance to say a few words to him in private. With three brothers, Stevie knew more than a little bit about how guys thought. As close as A.J. and Phil had always been, she suspected that it was probably hard for A.J. to admit his fears and weaknesses to another guy. Maybe he would have an easier time talking to her alone. As he shrugged on his backpack and prepared to mount, she cleared her throat. "So," she said casually. "What's new with you?"

"Not much." A.J. put his left foot in the stirrup and shoved off, swinging his right leg over and settling himself in the well-worn leather saddle. Gathering up the reins, he glanced over at Stevie. "Same old, same old."

"Oh." In the distance, Stevie heard her car door slam. Phil would be back any second. "Well, I just wanted to let you know, if there's anything you want to talk about . . . No pressure. I'm here, okay?"

A.J. shrugged. "Whatever." He busied himself with his stirrups, lengthening them by one hole each.

Stevie sighed. Obviously A.J. wasn't in the mood to chat at the moment. Still, she couldn't help feeling optimistic now that they were getting started on their ride. Seeing A.J. in the saddle, fiddling with his stirrups like a normal person, gave her hope that he was going to be all right. Maybe all he'd needed was time to adjust to his new reality. Stevie could understand that. She was sure it would have thrown her for a loop if she'd suddenly discovered something so earth-shattering about her own family.

Maybe he's coming around now, though, she thought. *He's definitely acting a lot more normal today than he has been lately.*

Soon Phil rejoined them, toting the pack Stevie had borrowed from Max. Strapping it on behind Teddy's saddle, he mounted and picked up the reins. "All set?"

"Let's go," Stevie and A.J. said in unison.

The three of them set out, crossing the courtyard and then following the dirt path between two of Cross County's smaller pastures. After crossing a small paved road and passing a field full of grazing sheep, they entered the outskirts of the state forest on a wide, well-traveled trail leading through a shrub-studded meadow. Ahead, Stevie could see the forest thickening gradually as it rose up the gentle foothills of the small mountains that began a few miles from Cross County. Even though Stevie knew that the forest was the same one that stretched to the north all the way to Pine Hollow, she always thought it looked a lot different here. Wilder, more exciting, and a little threatening at times. She shivered with anticipation, almost forgetting about A.J.'s problems for a moment as she simply looked forward to the ride.

For the next few minutes, the sounds of birds calling to each other mixed with the soft *thud-thud* of the horses' hooves as they walked. Nobody spoke, and Stevie suspected that the two guys were enjoying themselves as much as she was. The sun was bright overhead, and the air was that temperature that felt like no temperature at all, though beneath it Stevie could sense the brisk November cold just waiting to sweep in when the sun set.

Phil was the first to break the silence. "Check it out, Stevie," he commented, glancing at his friends' horses. "I think Blue is feeling her oats. Looks like she wants to race."

Stevie realized she hadn't been paying much attention to her mount. But now she saw that Blue had edged closer to Crystal, her ears pricked forward alertly and her attention on the other gray mare, who was returning the look. Both of the mares were moving faster than Teddy, who was ambling along a short distance behind them.

A.J. noticed, too. "What do you say, Stevie?" he said with a grin. "Feel up to a little friendly competition?"

"Anytime," Stevie replied immediately. "Let's go, you and me. First one to that big dead pine stump wins. Just name your gait."

"We'll keep it easy. Trot," A.J. replied.

The word was hardly out of his mouth when Stevie signaled her horse for the faster gait. Blue responded right away, swinging into a choppy but quick trot. Crystal snorted as A.J. urged her forward, and she quickly lengthened her stride to match Blue's pace. Stevie grinned at A.J., enjoying the feel of the crisp breeze on her face.

"You're dead meat, McDonnell!" she called.

"No way," A.J. cried in return. "We're an un-beatable team. Eat our dust!"

He urged Crystal forward even faster. Stevie leaned forward, calling encouraging words to Blue. The two mares were neck and neck as they detoured around a large patch of thorny wild rosebushes and aimed at the familiar landmark of a weather-beaten stump that had once been a huge pine.

Crystal was slightly ahead as they approached, and Stevie resisted the impulse to try any harder to catch up. She could be pretty competitive, but she didn't mind letting A.J. win this one. He needed it more than she did. As the two horses passed the stump, Crystal was a neck ahead. A.J. let out a whoop of triumph and pumped one fist in the air.

Stevie grinned and reached up to tip her riding helmet to him. "Nice going," she said. "We'll get you next time, though."

Phil cantered up on Teddy. "Are you two finished goofing around?" he asked, pretending to be stern. "Can we continue our ride now?"

"Sure, Dad." A.J. winked at Stevie. "Hold on a sec, though, okay? All that racing made me thirsty."

"Give me a break," Phil said. "Crystal was the one doing all the work."

"I know." Reaching around to unzip the top

closure of his backpack, A.J. pulled out a Thermos bottle. "It made me thirsty just watching her."

Stevie felt a sharp, sudden stab of suspicion. The last time A.J. and Phil had hung out together, A.J. had brought along a flask of liquor and spiked his soda. Did he have something similar in mind for today? "Hey," she said as casually as she could manage. "I don't feel like digging out my soda. Can I have a sip of yours?"

"Sure," A.J. said. "But it's not soda." He held out the Thermos.

Stevie felt her heart stop. "Um, what is it then?" she asked carefully, taking Blue's reins in one hand as she accepted the Thermos. Beside her, she could sense that Phil, too, was tense and paying close attention, waiting for A.J.'s response.

"It's that new fruit drink," A.J. replied, wiping his lips with the back of one riding glove. "You know, the one that hockey player advertises on TV? It's called Tooty Fruity."

"Oh." Stevie immediately felt foolish. "Right, I've had that before. Alex drinks it sometimes." Still, she lifted the Thermos to her lips and took a quick drink. The flavors of apple, cherry, and kiwi, strongly laced with sugar, flooded her taste buds. It was definitely Tooty Fruity—there was no mistaking the taste.

She handed the Thermos back to A.J., carefully avoiding Phil's gaze. If the two of them started trading meaningful glances, A.J. was sure to notice. Then they could forget about getting him to talk to them.

"Thanks," she told A.J. "That hit the spot."

A.J. nodded, took another long, thirsty swig, and then replaced the Thermos in his bag. "Okay," he said. "Now let's hit the trail!"

EIGHT

"Hi," Alex said when Lisa opened the door. "Wow, you look amazing!"

Lisa smiled, suddenly feeling a bit shy. She glanced down self-consciously at her slim black pants and pale blue fitted sweater, which flattered her slender figure and delicate coloring. "Thanks," she said. "You don't look so bad yourself."

"Aw, this old thang?" Alex joked, waving a hand at his usual outfit of jeans, sneakers, and a rugby shirt.

"I'm not talking about your clothes," Lisa replied, stepping out onto the front porch and pulling the door closed behind her. "I'm talking about you."

"Ah," Alex said, taking one of her hands in his own and tugging her gently toward him. "I see."

Lisa closed her eyes as he kissed her. *This is*

what I've been missing, she thought. *This is what I need.*

When they pulled apart, though, Lisa still felt oddly unsettled, as though there were something else they should be saying or doing to mark the occasion. Doing her best to ignore that feeling, she jangled her car keys in front of him. "Ready to go?"

"Like Freddie," he replied, stepping aside to let her walk beside him down the narrow front walk. He cast her a sidelong glance as they reached the car. "By the way . . ." He paused and cleared his throat. "I just want you to know—I've been thinking about you a lot for the past few days. More than usual, even, I mean. I hope you're doing okay."

Lisa knew he was thinking of Prancer. She smiled at him gratefully, reaching out to brush a loose eyelash off his cheek. "I'm trying," she said. "Thanks. I'll let you know if I need to talk, okay?"

He nodded, looking slightly relieved. They had reached the car, so he opened the driver's side door for her and then went around to the passenger's side and slid in himself.

Lisa started the car and backed out of the driveway. Turning toward town, she felt herself relax. It was crazy to feel as if she were escaping from her problems, but she couldn't help it. At least for a few hours, she wouldn't have to deal with her parents or sit alone and think about Prancer. She could just enjoy herself and have fun with Alex.

"Okay," she told him, glancing over as she drove. "This is your last chance to back out— otherwise we're headed to the museum."

"Drive on," Alex replied cheerfully. "I can't wait to get to the good old Wicma."

Lisa grinned at his use of the local nickname for the Willow Creek Museum of Art, or the WCMA. Despite its rather grand name, the museum was really just a few rooms in a Victorian mansion near the business district that housed a small permanent collection of local paintings and sculpture along with changing exhibitions of works loaned by wealthy patrons and other small regional museums.

A few minutes later Lisa pulled into a free parking space on the quiet, shady street where the museum stood. She and Alex got out of the car and strolled up the cobblestone walk arm in arm.

Lisa sighed happily when she saw the poster advertising the current special exhibition of modern sculpture. When she was younger, Lisa had taken art classes—sculpting, drawing, watercolor painting, and more. The only art form she still practiced on a regular basis was photography, but all those classes had left her with a real appreciation for all the visual arts. She loved spending a free afternoon wandering around a museum, whether it was the National Gallery in nearby Washington, D.C., or just the WCMA. It didn't even matter if she'd seen every painting in a gallery many times before. She always seemed to find something new to observe.

Unfortunately, despite her best efforts to educate him, Alex didn't share her fascination. He had a pretty good ear for music, but the visual arts left him cold. Lisa was happy that he cared enough about her to accompany her to the museum that day, and she vowed to return the favor by not making them stay too long.

"Let's go straight to the new exhibition, okay?" she suggested as they entered the cool, dim tiled entryway of the old mansion. Other than an elderly woman paging through a magazine behind the ticket table, the place was empty. "I don't feel like seeing anything else today."

Alex nodded agreeably, then stepped forward to pay their entrance fees. "Okay," he said, rejoining Lisa a moment later. "Let's go see us some art!"

Lisa rolled her eyes apologetically at the woman behind the ticket table, hoping she didn't think Alex was making fun of the museum. Then she followed him into the front gallery, formerly the double parlor of the big old house. Nobody else was inside, and their footsteps echoed off the gleaming tile floor.

Several sculptors were represented in the exhibition, most of them from northern Virginia or the surrounding areas. Lisa took Alex's hand and wandered toward the first piece, a large twisted-metal sculpture displayed on a low pedestal.

"Whoa," Alex said, cocking his head to one side and examining it. "Looks like this one got run over by somebody's car on its way here."

"Very funny." Lisa stuck out her tongue at him, then turned back toward the piece. "I like it. It has a lot of energy, don't you think?"

"Maybe if you pushed it down a hill," Alex joked. He dropped her hand and left her side to wander around and look at some of the other pieces.

Lisa moved around the room more slowly, gazing at each sculpture and reading the accompanying signs. When she caught up with Alex he was standing in front of a massive red clay piece. Lisa glanced at it and blinked. The sculpture seemed to portray two figures, their plump red limbs intertwined suggestively.

"Yikes," she said with a slightly embarrassed laugh. "Is that what I think it is?"

Alex grinned and pointed to the sign, which proclaimed that the piece was titled *In the Flesh*.

"I'm no art critic," he said. "But I know what I like." He leered at her playfully and slipped one arm around her shoulders. "So," he said, squeezing her tight. "Does it give you any ideas?"

Lisa wriggled free, glancing around to make sure nobody was watching. "Ha ha," she told him pertly. "Come on, let's keep moving."

Alex laughed, then trailed after her as she continued making her way around the room. When they had checked out the entire exhibition, Lisa glanced at her watch.

"Ready to go?" she asked Alex. "We can head over to the mall and buy your shoes before dinner if you want."

"Sounds good," Alex agreed. "Let's motor."

It was a fifteen-minute drive from the museum to the Willow Creek mall on the outskirts of town. Lisa and Alex spent the first couple of minutes of the ride chatting about the art exhibition. Then Alex asked Lisa about her day at school.

Lisa shrugged. "It was fine," she said. "The usual. Well, except that my English teacher has gone totally insane. Not only did we just turn in a paper on *Frankenstein* today—now she wants us to read *Ethan Frome* over Thanksgiving break and write a five-pager on it by the time we get back."

She regretted the words immediately. *Why did*

I have to bring up Thanksgiving? she wondered as she glanced over and saw Alex frown slightly. He'd always had trouble with her visits to California—partly because he hated being separated from her for any length of time, and partly because he was jealous of her friendship with Skye Ransom, an actor who lived near her father in Los Angeles.

"My teachers are assigning tons of stuff for the break, too," Alex said carefully, keeping his gaze trained out the windshield. "Of course, it's not really a problem for me. I'll have plenty of time to do it, hanging around home all week."

"Uh-huh." Gripping the steering wheel tightly, Lisa searched for a good way to change the subject quickly. The last thing she wanted to do was turn their relaxed, pleasant date into some kind of tense standoff. "Um, so did Stevie go over to see Phil and A.J.?"

Alex nodded. "Yeah, she left just before I came over to get you," he reported, sounding relieved at the new topic. "She seems pretty worried about A.J."

"I don't blame her," Lisa said, her grip on the wheel relaxing. Obviously Alex had no more interest in fighting about her trip to California than she did. That was a good sign. "I mean, I know he had a lot to drink at the party at your house. But it wasn't until I saw him sitting at the

116

bar in that college restaurant that I started to wonder if there was a real problem. You know?"

"Sure. But you know Stevie. She's determined to ride in on her white horse"—he laughed—"literally, except for the white part—and fix everything."

"Maybe she can do it," Lisa said optimistically. "I really think it would help A.J. a lot if he would just open up and trust somebody with what he's feeling. And if there's one thing your sister is good at, it's getting people to talk to her."

At that moment, Stevie was beginning to wonder if A.J. was ever going to shut up about his girlfriend, Julianna, and her upcoming role in some school play. They had been riding for almost an hour and were deep in the woods, following a winding trail that meandered along beside the river. At first the three of them had talked casually about school and other general subjects. But then A.J. had taken over the conversation, insisting on sharing every detail of Julianna's victorious tryout. Stevie was starting to feel impatient—so far, the topic of A.J.'s adoption hadn't even come up. Neither had his recent drinking spree. Maybe those things weren't at the front of A.J.'s mind at the moment, but they were all Stevie could think about.

"Come on," she said, interrupting a monologue about Julianna's wonderful singing voice, "I think the horses could use a rest and a drink. Why don't we stop and have dinner?"

"Good idea," Phil agreed quickly. He glanced down toward the river. "There's a spot just ahead with a nice view. We'll have to be careful, though—the current is kind of strong along here, so we shouldn't let the horses wade in too far."

"Yeah, good plan," A.J. said with a grin. "Especially since we totally forgot to bring their bathing suits, and I happen to know for a fact that there's no skinny-dipping allowed in the state park. Hyuk hyuk hyuk!"

Stevie shot him a quick glance. A.J. had always been something of a clown, but for the past few minutes, when he wasn't bragging about Julianna, he'd been making goofy comments that weren't really all that funny. If the temperature hadn't been so cool and pleasant, especially under the shade of the old-growth forest, she might have thought he was getting overheated and light-headed from exertion. "Speak for yourself," she said, deciding he was probably just letting off steam and acting silly. And where was the harm in that? "I have Blue's polka-dot bikini right here in my saddlebag."

A.J. thought about that for half a second.

Then he started laughing so hard that Stevie was afraid he was going to fall right out of the saddle. "Good one, Stevie!" A.J. hooted, slapping one hand on his knee so hard that Crystal flicked her ears back at the sound.

Stevie glanced over at Phil, who shrugged, looking worried. "Come on," he said. "I'll show you guys the spot I was talking about."

He led the way off the trail, pointing out a grassy clearing where they could let the horses rest after their drink. Ten minutes later the three of them were busy setting out their own picnic dinner on a rock overlooking a small, tumbling waterfall. The long ride had made Stevie hungry, and she spent the next few minutes focusing on the sandwiches and sodas she'd brought. But when her stomach had stopped grumbling, her attention turned back to A.J. So far the ride was a total bust. It was time for her to say something about the reason they were all out here, whether he wanted to hear it or not.

Taking a deep breath, Stevie decided to plunge right in. "Listen, A.J.," she said seriously. "Phil and I were hoping we'd get a chance to talk to you today. You know, about all the stuff that's been going on in your life lately. We know you aren't that psyched about discussing it with people, but we want to remind you that we're your friends. We care about you a lot, and we hate to think you may be hurting and there's nothing we can do to help."

She paused to see how A.J. was taking her words. The way he'd been acting lately, there was no telling how he might respond. But to her surprise, A.J. didn't seem to be paying attention. He was munching on potato chips, staring up at the sky blankly.

Phil noticed, too. "Yo," he said to A.J. "Did you hear what she just said?"

"Did I hear her? What am I, deaf?" A.J. let out a high-pitched giggle and rolled his eyes. "Come on, dude—you're her boyfriend. You know better than anyone that she's got the biggest mouth on the planet!"

Stevie wasn't sure quite how to take that. It certainly wasn't the reaction she'd been expecting, and judging by the perplexed expression on Phil's face, he felt the same way. Still, she plunged on with her speech. "So anyway, we just hope you'll come to us if you need to talk things through," she said. "We might not be able to understand exactly what you're going through, but we'll certainly try to be—"

She stopped short as A.J. tipped his head back and took another long swig from his Thermos. Suspicion crept through her veins like a sudden chill on a warm day. But she had tasted the contents of that Thermos herself. The only thing in it was the overly sweet fruit drink. At least that was all she'd tasted. . . .

At that moment Phil suddenly leaped forward. "Excuse me," he said grimly, snatching the Thermos before A.J. knew what was happening. "Let me see that."

"Hey!" A.J. cried. But he didn't seem very upset. In fact, he was grinning broadly. "If you want a sip, all you have to do is ask. You don't need to get grabby."

Phil ignored him. Raising the Thermos to his nose, he sniffed carefully. Then he shot A.J. an uncertain glance. "Smells like Tooty Fruity all right," he said. "Is that all that's in here?"

A.J. giggled again and squinched up his face— he'd never been able to manage a proper wink. "Well, now that you mention it," he said teasingly, "there was a bottle of vodka sitting around when I filled it. I suppose it's possible a few drops might have fallen in, purely by accident, of course."

Vodka! Stevie grimaced, realizing she'd been had. Vodka was flavorless—that was why she hadn't tasted it when she'd taken a sip earlier, especially in the strongly flavored fruit drink A.J. had used as a mixer.

All this time he's been guzzling his fruit cocktail right under our noses, she thought, watching as Phil tilted the Thermos and poured out the rest of the drink. Not much came out—A.J. had already swallowed most of it.

Stevie traded a grim look with Phil. Their plan had backfired in a big way. Not only was it useless to try to talk to A.J. now, but they were going to have to figure out a way to deal with the situation. They were on horseback, miles from civilization. Dusk would be falling before too much longer.

And A.J. was totally wasted.

NINE

Callie was focusing so intently on keeping her right leg straight in Windsor's stirrup that it took her a while to notice Ben Marlow, who was leaning on the top rail of the main schooling ring, watching her. When she finally saw him, she couldn't help feeling a little self-conscious. Normally she didn't care if people watched her sessions—Max regularly stopped by to check on her progress, and Carole, Stevie, and her other friends had come to lend their support often enough. But Ben had a way of looking at people that was a little disconcerting—his dark, serious eyes beneath their heavy brows never seemed to give away what he was thinking. Besides that, Callie was still smarting over Veronica's comments the day before in phys ed. It had never been easy for Callie to be the center of attention. She had missed inheriting that particular gene from her gregarious, spotlight-loving parents, though Scott had it in spades. The only time she was happy to have people looking at her, noticing her, praising her was after a race. That was when she knew she'd earned their attention, rather than commanding it simply by the coincidence of her birth.

It's not like Ben is the type of guy to be impressed by money or family connections, though, she reminded herself as she nudged Windsor and sent him slowly toward the gate. *So no big deal, right? Ben's just watching you, that's all.* She wondered if her upcoming return to Valley Vista had anything to do with her sudden paranoia. She suspected that it probably did.

When she reached Ben, she stopped Windsor, who put his head forward to nudge at the young stable hand's shoulder. Ben lifted one hand and rubbed the big gelding on his broad forehead, scratching him under his forelock. As always, Callie was amazed at the way the rather aloof gelding warmed up to Ben instantly—Ben really did have a magic touch, as she'd heard Max comment more than once.

"Hi," Callie greeted him.

"Looks like you're still having trouble with your balance," Ben said bluntly.

Callie blinked, immediately feeling a bit defensive. "Of course I am," she said. "My right leg is still weak, remember? Anyway, I'm getting better."

"Sure," Ben said, still rubbing Windsor's face. "But maybe not as fast as you could. Me, I'd try more work without stirrups. Might help you regain your natural feel for the seat instead of focusing on your legs."

Callie opened her mouth to reply sharply, then stopped to think about what Ben had said. She had to admit it made sense. She'd been working so hard on strengthening her weak leg, forcing it to carry its share of her weight, that she hadn't done much work on her balance. She knew she was overcompensating and throwing herself off, but until now she hadn't really stopped to think about how she could fix it.

"Thanks," she said slowly. "I'll try that." It was never easy for Callie to accept help from other people. Then again, Ben wasn't like most people: She had seen the way horses trusted him, and that made her trust him, too, at least when it came to riding advice. While he often seemed completely oblivious to the passions and concerns that motivated other people, nothing mattered more to him than doing the best thing for horses. In the past, his apparent lack of interest had often made Callie impatient, especially when she was trying to get information out of him. But now, for the first time, she was starting to understand, at least a little, what Carole saw in him. It was obvious to anyone with two eyes that

Carole and Ben had some kind of special connection, though it was just as clear that neither of them was in any hurry to do anything about it.

Callie couldn't really understand that—it just seemed like a waste of time to her. Two days earlier, she had noticed that Ben wasn't around when she came to Pine Hollow. The only reason she'd noticed it was that it made two days in a row, since Ben had actually taken Sunday off for once. Callie hadn't thought much about it at the time—she'd been way too focused on her own problems for that—but now she wondered if his absence had anything to do with Carole's banishment. She quickly dismissed that theory, though. It wasn't as if Ben would ever neglect his duties at the stable over something as insignificant as another person.

Too bad he can't be as open and caring with Carole as he is with horses, Callie mused as she dismounted and reached for the crutches Ben was handing her. *But then again, maybe it's just as well they never got anything going. It would just be one more thing for Carole to be missing right about now.*

As she thought it, she heard the sound of a truck shifting gears as it trundled up the stable drive. Glancing over her shoulder to make sure that the noise wasn't bothering Windsor, she saw that the gelding was munching peacefully on a mouthful of tall grass he'd swiped from beneath the fence. "Wonder who that is?" she commented, glancing over and noting that the vehicle was a large, multihorse transport trailer.

"Guess it's here for Samson," Ben replied.

"Samson?" Callie repeated, pulling off her hard hat and shaking out her long blond hair, which had been tucked up beneath it. Taking another look at the truck, she noticed that it had Canadian plates. "Oh, you mean his new owner's picking him up already?"

Ben shrugged. "He was on his way back from another show. Made sense."

Callie couldn't argue with that. Samson was a fantastic horse, with a promising future in the show ring. It was no big shock that his new owner wanted to get right to work with him.

I wonder if Carole knows, she thought. *I wonder if anyone told her he's leaving today.*

She had hardly finished the thought when she caught a flash of movement out of the corner of her eye. Glancing toward it, she saw a small, jeans-clad figure crouched in the shadowy corner between the stable wall and the large evergreen shrub that hid the building's gas meter. Callie winced as the figure leaned forward a little, revealing its identity. Carole was clearly doing her best not to be seen as she watched Max lead

Samson out of the stable entrance. Her face wore a haunted expression and her posture was nervous and tense.

Callie quickly averted her gaze from Carole as Max led Samson toward the big horse van. The gelding was dressed in quilted standing bandages and a poll guard, covered with a padded blanket, and his flowing black tail was enclosed in a bright pink wrap—all of which vaguely gave him the look of a frumpy, bathrobed housewife. Even so, he looked as magnificent and regal as always. Pausing halfway across the stable yard, he let out a loud snort and lifted his head to sniff the air curiously. Max waited patiently at his head, letting the horse come along at his own pace. It was obvious that Samson realized something unusual was happening—his nostrils were flared, and his eyes were bright and curious as he stepped forward, seeming to dance lightly on his toes.

Even though she had no real personal connection to Samson, Callie felt tears welling up. He really was an incredible horse, and her heart ached on Carole's behalf. *If he were mine,* she thought, *in heart if not in fact, I could never stand to lose him.*

"Be tough to see him go," Ben said abruptly.

Callie started. She had almost forgotten he was still standing beside her. She wasn't quite sure what he meant by his comment. But she guessed he was having some of the same thoughts she was, whether or not he'd actually seen Carole hiding across the stable yard. "Uh-huh," she replied. "He's some horse."

Callie risked another quick peek at Carole. She was still in the same position, her intense gaze never wavering from Samson as he stepped toward the ramp that someone had just lowered off the back of the van. Callie wished there was something she could do to help—she knew that Carole felt her emotions intensely, and she had to be right in the middle of a big hurt right about then. But there was no way Callie could go to her without giving her away to Max. Besides, Callie suspected that this might be something Carole had to go through alone.

It didn't take long for Max and the van's driver to load Samson. All too soon they were raising the ramp and securing the rear door. After a last quick consultation with Max, the driver climbed back into the cab, slowly turned, and pulled down the gravel drive.

Good-bye, Samson, Callie thought, blinking back a tear. She didn't glance at Carole's hiding place again, but she was imagining what she must be feeling at that very moment, as the van's turn signal winked on and it lumbered out onto the road and away from Pine Hollow. *We'll miss you.*

She was still thinking about Carole as she led Windsor into the stable building. Ben wandered along with her, though he hadn't said a word in several minutes.

Poor Carole, Callie thought. *She really has it tough right now. I wonder if being away from the stable will make it easier or harder to get over Samson.*

She didn't wonder about it for long, though. At that moment someone called her name from across the stable entryway. Glancing up, she saw George hurrying toward her with a pleased grin.

"Hey, Callie!" he exclaimed. He sounded so thrilled to see her that a stranger might have thought they hadn't set eyes on each other in months, rather than having run into each other half a dozen times earlier that day in school. "How's it going?"

For a second Callie dared to hope that Ben's presence beside her might discourage George from hanging around too long. He hardly noticed when her girlfriends were with her, but the presence of other guys often seemed to intimidate him.

But her hope faded quickly. "Uh, okay," Ben muttered, already moving away in the direction of the stable office. "Later."

Callie did her best not to grimace as he disappeared, leaving her alone with George. Grasping

Windsor's lead line tightly, she cleared her throat meaningfully. "I'd better move along, too," she told George. "I've got to get Windsor cleaned up and put away or I'll be late for dinner."

"No problem." George beamed at her. "I'll help you. That way you'll get finished faster."

Callie couldn't think of anything to say that wouldn't sound mean, so she kept quiet and nodded helplessly. As she led Windsor across the entryway toward the stable aisle, George kept pace with her, chattering about endurance riding. From what Callie could gather, he'd looked up some information about the sport on the Internet and was eager to share what he'd learned.

They had almost reached Windsor's stall when Callie spotted Polly Giacomin rounding the corner toward them at the end of the aisle. Feeling desperate, she interrupted George's monologue. "Hey, Polly!" she called, waving her down. "What's up?"

Polly looked a little surprised that Callie was greeting her so enthusiastically, but she hurried toward her. "Not much," she said agreeably. Casting a curious glance at George, she added, "What's up with you?"

Callie just shrugged in response. "Hey, did you see Samson leave just now?" she asked, fishing for a topic that might keep Polly around to serve as a buffer between her and George.

"Uh-huh. I helped Red put the bandages on him," Polly reported. "Pretty big news, hmm? Samson going off to be a superstar in Canada, I mean."

Out of the corner of her eye, Callie saw that George was shifting his weight from one foot to the other, looking a bit uncomfortable. Ignoring the twinge of guilt she felt about what she was doing, she nodded. "Definitely big news," she agreed. "But sad news for us here at Pine Hollow, right?"

"For sure. Especially for Carole. I don't think she knew he was leaving today," Polly confided. "I saw her as we were leaving school, and she looked kind of freaked when I mentioned it. I guess she was bummed that she couldn't be here to see him off."

"Hmm." Callie wasn't about to give away the fact that Carole had snuck in for one last good-bye, no matter how desperate she was to keep Polly interested in the conversation. "So listen, Polly. I've been meaning to ask you about that neck collar I saw you carrying the other day. Are you training Romeo to drive?"

She did her best to look interested as Polly happily launched into a description of her latest training plans for her gelding. Callie's first impression that Polly was a bit of a space cadet hadn't changed over the months of their acquaintance. But right at that moment, she was glad of the other girl's incessant chattiness. Sneaking a quick peek at George, she saw that he was already looking bored and restless.

Again Callie felt a touch of guilt. Lately it seemed she would try just about anything to blow him off short of just telling him the truth. But she was getting sick and tired of wondering how to treat George when they were alone together and worrying about hurting his feelings.

So from now on, she told herself, leading Windsor into his stall as Polly leaned against the wall just outside and chattered on, *I'll just have to make sure that we're not alone if I can help it.* It didn't occur to her that she had already tried that and it hadn't worked so far.

Carole was relieved to see that her father's car wasn't in the garage when she got home a few minutes later. She pulled her car into its usual spot, offering a silent prayer of thanks that she hadn't gotten into an accident on her way home, despite the hot tears that had been blurring her vision since she'd snuck away from Pine Hollow.

I can't believe he's gone, she thought, remembering the way Samson had stood in the stable doorway, proud and alert. He had searched the air with his flared nostrils, almost as if he were looking for someone . . . for her? Could it be possible that he would miss her even a tenth as much as she would miss him?

She didn't know. But one thing was certain— she was glad she'd gotten to see him one last time. She knew that her father, Max, and Dr. Durbin would stand in line to strangle her if they knew she'd faked a stomachache and sneaked over to Pine Hollow. But she didn't care. It had been worth it, even if it meant getting grounded for the rest of her high-school career. Even if her father never spoke to her again . . .

Pushing aside that last thought, Carole hurried into the house and up the stairs. Now that the joy of seeing Samson was starting to wear off, her general depression about everything else in her life was coming back full force. This was it. She'd said her last good-byes, to Pine Hollow as well as to Samson, and she was just going to have to face it.

How do other people do it? she wondered as she headed into her room. *How do they get up every day, eat breakfast, and go to school and do homework and all the rest of it, when they don't have a trip to the stable to look forward to, a visit with a special horse or a nice long trail ride to make the day worthwhile?*

Closing her bedroom door behind her, Carole headed straight for the pine bookcase beneath the window. Several photo albums were stacked on the bottom shelf, and Carole picked up the red one on the top of the pile. Sitting down cross-legged on the floor, she set the album on her lap and flipped it open to the first page. A shot of Samson flying over a plain rail fence in the schooling ring jumped out at her.

Carole couldn't help smiling when she saw it. Lisa had snapped the photo a month or two earlier as part of a project for the photography club she belonged to, and she had given Carole a spare print. The photo caught the big black horse right at the peak of the jump, and it captured all his power and his joy in the exercise. Carole herself was visible only as a tucked-in figure on his back, dwarfed by her mount's size and sheer personality. Like all the time she'd spent with Samson, she remembered that moment as if it had happened just that day.

Flipping slowly through the album, Carole looked at other pictures of Samson. She also lingered over the many photos of Starlight, as well as those of some of the other Pine Hollow horses. Now that she was banished from their world, it looked even more wonderful and enticing than usual. She missed it so much already that she didn't know if she could stand it.

As she turned to a new page, she saw a photo she'd all but forgotten. It was one that Max had asked his wife to take the previous spring, a group shot of Pine Hollow's staff. Carole was standing in the front row between Denise and a part-time stable hand named Aurora who'd gone away to college that fall. Behind them were Max, Red, and the others. Off to one side, almost as if he'd wandered into the picture by accident, was Ben.

As soon as she saw him, Carole's thoughts twisted in a slightly different direction. Even through her grief and her intense focus on Samson, she hadn't been able to avoid noticing Ben. The only thing that had distracted her the slightest bit from the big black horse was spotting Ben over by the schooling ring. He'd been standing with Callie and Windsor, watching Max load Samson into the van. He hadn't seen Carole, but she'd had a clear view of him.

Playing with one corner of the album page beneath her hand, Carole pictured Ben's intense gaze as he leaned forward and kissed her. . . . Then, just as clearly, she saw his indifferent look as they passed in the stable aisle just a few hours later.

She sighed with frustration, embarrassment, and a whole mix of other emotions that she couldn't be bothered to identify. It just didn't make any sense. She still had no idea what to think of what had happened between them.

And seeing Ben standing there in the stable yard a few minutes earlier, talking with Callie and patting Windsor as if he didn't even notice that Carole wasn't around anymore, definitely didn't help her come any closer to figuring it out.

TEN

"This isn't funny, A.J.!" Stevie exclaimed. "What were you thinking?"

A.J. shrugged and leaned back on their picnic blanket. Just in the nick of time, Stevie reached beneath his back and grabbed the sharp Swiss Army knife she'd brought to slice cheese and apples. In his condition, A.J. could easily have leaned on it and hurt himself without even noticing. She moved a little too fast, though, and the knife caught on the long tails of his flannel shirt, ripping a small slash in the fabric. "Oops," she muttered.

"Why think?" A.J. murmured, paying no attention to what she'd done. Tucking his hands behind his head, he gazed up peacefully at the tree branches far above. "Too much trouble."

Shooting a guilty glance at Phil, who also hadn't noticed the accident, Stevie flipped the blade closed and tucked it in the front pocket of her jeans. Then she returned her attention to

A.J. She and Phil had been trying to talk to him for the past few minutes, but he refused to take anything they said seriously. The initial giddiness was wearing off a little, and he seemed to be getting sleepy and distracted. *What are we going to do now?* she wondered. *Instead of helping him by bringing him out here, I'm starting to think we just made things worse!*

Phil gave A.J. a hard shove on the shoulder. "Wake up," he said sharply. "Stevie's right. This is serious. You've got to get a grip."

A.J. closed his eyes. "Don't be such a spoilsport," he said with a heavy sigh.

Stevie took a deep breath, reminding herself to be patient. It was like Max was always telling them—when a horse made a mistake during a lesson, it was usually because it didn't understand what it was supposed to be doing. A rider wouldn't accomplish anything positive by yelling at the animal or hitting it. By the same token, she couldn't just let herself blow up at A.J., as tempted as she was to do so. That might scare him off from ever talking to her about his problems.

"Look," she said as gently as she could. "I know this is a tough time for you, A.J. You just found out your whole family, your whole past, everything is different from what you thought it was. You just realized that the people you trusted most in the world have been lying to you—maybe they didn't really see it that way, but still, there it is. So now you have to figure out how to act and how to handle it all. I can't even imagine what that would be like."

"No," A.J. said quietly. "You can't." He was still looking up at the trees, but now his expression was more remote, as if he were actually staring at something far, far above them. "But I can tell you, it really sucks."

Stevie held her breath. *I think that's one of the most honest things A.J. has said to anyone since this whole mess started,* she thought.

"We hear you," Phil told his friend. "And we want to help. We really do."

A.J. shrugged. "Yeah, well, that's nice and all," he said. "But there's not much you can do, you know? I mean, it's not like anyone can change the past. I just wish I could forget about it. Things were a lot easier before I knew."

"I'm sure that's true," Stevie said. "But what's done is done. Now you've got to figure out how to deal with it."

A.J. turned and blinked at her. "But what if I don't want to deal with it? Can't I just forget it ever happened?" He sighed and answered his own question. "No way. There's no way I can forget, no matter how hard I try. Like I said, it sucks."

Stevie was glad that A.J. was finally opening up a little. But as he blinked at her again, suddenly looking rather sleepy and out of it, she couldn't help wondering if they were really making any kind of breakthrough.

After all, she told herself, *this won't change a thing if he doesn't remember any of it once his buzz wears off.*

Lisa chewed her onion ring slowly and glanced at Alex, who was sitting across from her at the round metal food-court table. He was busily picking the lettuce off his club sandwich, and that seemed to require all his concentration. At least Lisa hoped that was why neither of them had said a word in the past two or three minutes.

It was weird. One of the nicest things about being with Alex had always been that the two of them never ran out of things to say to each other. Even when there was nothing in particular going on in their lives, they had been happy to discuss silly things, like what they would take with them to a deserted island. Or they could spend the better part of an evening finding new and creative ways to compliment each other, or coming up with goofy pet names, or talking about what kind of house they might like to live in someday. But now, even after being apart for the better part of the past month, it seemed that they had already run out of topics of conversation.

She had first noticed it half an hour earlier when Alex had been trying on basketball shoes at the sporting-goods store in another part of the mall. As she watched him lace up pair after pair of sneakers, she'd actually started to feel a bit bored. It was an odd feeling, and one she'd never thought she would feel as long as she and Alex were together.

What's with me today? she wondered, reaching for another onion ring. *It's not as if there's nothing to talk about these days. It's just that it seems like we've already covered them all.*

She thought back to their conversation earlier in the day. On the ride over to the mall, after that little near argument about her Thanksgiving plans and their brief chat about A.J., they had spent the next few miles discussing the trig test Alex had taken that day at school. Next they had speculated a little more about Stevie and Phil's progress with A.J. out on the trails behind Cross County. By that time they'd reached the mall, and soon afterward the conversation had tapered off. Aside from a lengthy discussion of whether they should head back into town to their favorite burger place or just pick up something at the mall food court, they hadn't found much to talk about that could hold their attention for more than a minute or two.

I guess the problem is that most of the important topics just don't seem safe right now, Lisa thought, dabbing grease off her chin with a napkin. *I mean, the last thing I want to do is bring up my trip to California again. Alex has never exactly been reasonable about that particular subject, and I'm already feeling weird about it myself because of this whole college thing.*

Unfortunately, her decision about where to go to college was another topic that she didn't feel completely comfortable discussing with Alex. When she'd first told him of her choice to attend NVU, he had been really supportive, just as she had expected. But since then he'd made a few comments about it that made her think that maybe he wasn't behind her a hundred percent after all. He always backed away from the remarks, so she still wasn't sure what was bugging him about it. And she wasn't sure that she really wanted to know. It was all she could do to deal with her parents' disapproval as it was.

As she was thinking about all the lectures she was in for when her father got hold of her, she suddenly felt something nudging at her shin. "Eep!" she cried, startled, as she automatically jerked her foot back.

When she glanced across the table, she saw

that Alex was grinning at her mischievously. "What?" he said with mock surprise. "You mean you aren't up for a little footsie?"

Lisa relaxed, then laughed. Slipping off one of her flats, she reached across the space beneath the table until she found Alex's leg. Wriggling her stockinged foot between his high-top and the hem of his jeans, she tweaked him with her toes. "You mean like this?"

Alex scooted his chair around the table until he was right next to her. "Actually, let's forget about footsie, my beautiful mall rat," he murmured, slipping one arm around her waist and lifting his other hand to her chin, tilting her face toward his. "Did you ever wonder what it's like to kiss a guy with bacon breath?"

Lisa smiled as her lips met his. Letting her eyes close, she forgot all about her worries. Who needed constant conversation when they still had wonderful romantic moments like these?

"So what should we do?" Phil muttered. "He just about finished off that Thermos. And for a while there I thought he was going to pass out right on top of the food. I'm starting to think he's too toasted to ride, especially on these trails."

Stevie glanced over at A.J., who was licking potato chip crumbs off his fingers and offering a piece of apple to Crystal with his other hand. It had been Stevie's brilliant idea to drop the apple slice on the ground as a pretense for insisting that A.J. go over and feed it to the horses. That way she and Phil could hold a quick, private conference back at the picnic area. After his comments about the adoption a few minutes earlier, A.J. hadn't been very interested in talking about himself. He'd returned to praising Julianna for a while, describing her amazing singing voice again before slipping into a garbled medley of favorite Broadway show tunes.

"I know," Stevie said worriedly. "Maybe it wouldn't be such a bad thing if he took a nap before we head back." She glanced at the sky, noting the pink cast of the clouds as the sun sank slowly toward the tree line. "A short one, I mean. Or maybe one of us should lead Crystal, and—"

Before she could finish the sentence, a loud snort cut her off. It was Crystal. The mare was tossing her head, clearly startled by the fact that A.J. was now hanging off the side of her saddle, clinging to the cantle and doing his best to clamber aboard.

"A.J.!" Phil shouted, jumping to his feet. "What are you doing?"

A.J.'s hand slipped, and for a second Stevie thought he was going to fall. But then he got a grip on the pommel with one hand and a fistful of Crystal's wavy pale mane with the other. Heaving himself upward, he managed to get each of his legs on the proper side of the mare's saddle. Then he grabbed the reins and glanced over at Stevie and Phil with a grin. "Yeee-hah!" he whooped. "Let's see if you slowpokes can catch us this time!" He kicked Crystal sharply in the side and snapped his reins like a cowboy in a cheesy Western, at the same time letting out another shrill whoop.

With pounding hooves, Crystal broke from a dead halt into a gallop and raced down the trail, sending twigs and stones flying in every direction. A.J.'s giddy cries drifted back to Stevie and Phil as they stared after him, too frozen with surprise and horror to move.

ELEVEN

"Here, let me carry that," George said as Callie grabbed her backpack off the bench in the locker room and swung toward the door. "It looks too heavy for you to manage with your crutches."

Callie had to stop herself from rolling her eyes at George's offer. She had come straight to Pine Hollow after school, so her bag was packed with several textbooks as well as her purse and a few other items. It was pretty heavy, but it certainly wasn't anything she couldn't handle.

"Thanks," she said, biting back a more irritated response. "But I've got it covered." Before George could protest, she stopped and leaned on one crutch while she shrugged the backpack on over her shoulders.

George watched her, looking concerned, but he didn't say another word about it. Instead he pointed forward as they continued on their way.

"Watch it," he said as they approached the

stable entrance. "Looks like somebody needs to get out the pooper scooper. Don't step in it."

Oh, please? Can't I? Callie thought sarcastically, glancing down briefly at the pile of fresh manure just inside the door. But she just smiled tightly at George. "Right. Thanks." Polly had departed a little while earlier despite Callie's best efforts, and George had insisted on helping her finish up with Windsor. Now he was walking her out to the stable yard to wait for Scott to pick her up.

George smiled back, not seeming to notice her irritation. "Sure," he said. "Here, let me hold the door for you."

Callie swung out into the pinkish late-afternoon light. She was starting to wonder if she was going to have to put up with George sticking to her like glue for the rest of her high-school career. He certainly didn't seem to be getting bored with following her around.

"Watch it!" George said urgently. He pointed out a rough spot ahead where Samson's horse trailer had kicked up some gravel. It was at least five feet away, but that didn't stop him from taking her arm and steering her in a broad circle around it.

Callie gritted her teeth, reminding herself that he meant well. What was her problem, anyway? She always reacted as if George were some kind of criminal for being concerned about her leg or her well-being. She shouldn't get down on him for wanting to help her.

It's more than that, though, she thought. *It's almost like he gets a kick out of my being helpless.*

That idea made her decidedly uncomfortable. She glanced at him sidelong. For all George's faults, she had always thought of him as a good person. But what kind of good person wanted to see someone else helpless?

Don't get paranoid, kiddo, she told herself sternly. *You're just annoyed with George right now because he's doing the leech act, so you're looking for things to pick on about him. Making things up out of thin air. Right?*

Fortunately, Scott's green sports car wheeled into Pine Hollow's driveway at that moment, distracting Callie from her speculation. "There's my ride," she told George, relieved. "See you in school."

She hurried to meet Scott before he could turn into the small parking area to the left of the drive. "Whoa! Where's the fire?" Scott joked as Callie flagged him down, opened the door, and slung her crutches and backpack into the front seat. "I thought I'd have to hang around here for ages waiting for you to get finished. I almost brought a book."

"Nope, I'm ready." Callie climbed in and yanked the door shut. "Let's hit it."

Scott shrugged and spun the wheel to turn the car around. Callie glanced back at George one last time as they headed down the driveway. He waved when he saw her looking, and she lifted one hand to wave back weakly, trying to ignore the weird, oddly protective expression on his round face.

When she got home a few minutes later, Callie headed straight up to her room. She was still feeling unsettled by her latest encounter with George, though she wasn't sure why.

But she knew one thing. She wanted to get rid of her crutches as soon as possible. Not just because of what people back in Valley Vista might say. But because she was sick of feeling as if she wasn't fully in control of her own body. She was sick of being at the mercy of those stupid, ugly hunks of metal she'd been lugging around for the past several months.

Maybe George will get over it when I can walk and run and ride just as well as he can, she thought irritably. *Maybe then he'll go find some other helpless girl to follow around with his big, moony puppy-dog eyes.*

After checking to make sure her bedroom door was closed tight, Callie swung over to her desk. Leaning her crutches against it, she gripped the back of her desk chair and took a deep breath. She looked across the room at her bed. Her goal.

"Here goes nothing," she muttered.

Then she pushed off, stepping forward first with her left leg. One step. Two. Her right leg quivered but held her up. Three steps. She was almost halfway there.

Ha! she thought fiercely. *Check this out, George. Looks like I don't need you hanging around helping me anym—*

At that moment she put her weight on her right leg again—a little too hard, too fast. She felt herself start to overbalance and tilt sideways, her ankle wobbling wildly. She windmilled her arms, trying to recover.

But it was too late. Her ankle gave out, twisting to the side. She fell forward and almost wiped out on the hardwood. By catching herself and shoving hard with her good leg, she managed to flop forward and land heavily on the end of the bed instead. Her elbow hit the bedpost with a loud smack, the impact making her whole arm go numb for a couple of seconds.

She yelped in pain, then crawled forward until she was lying facedown in the middle of the bed. Clenching both hands into fists, she pounded on her bedspread with all her strength, tears of frustration springing to her eyes. Wasn't she ever going to get her body back?

"One-two-three-four. Five-six-seven-eight. Kick. Back. Kick. Back," Carole panted under her breath, moving along to the beat of the aerobics tape on her portable stereo.

It was almost dinnertime, and she knew she ought to go downstairs and start cooking. Her father was due home any moment, and if Carole wanted to get back in his good graces, a nice hot bowl of pasta or platter of his favorite barbecued pork chops could only help the cause.

But she couldn't work up enough enthusiasm to go down and get started. *After all, what's the point in trying to get back to Pine Hollow sooner?* she thought gloomily. *It won't make any difference. Samson still won't be there.*

Even as she thought it, she knew she was being melodramatic. Pine Hollow meant everything to her, with or without Samson. She had friends there, a job, and lots of other wonderful horses to care for—not least among them her own faithful gelding, Starlight. But it had been a really long, difficult day, and she couldn't help indulging in self-pity for a little while, even as she kept kicking and lunging automatically to the aerobics instructor's shouted instructions.

Just then she heard a faint ringing sound over

the pounding beat of the music. The phone. She was tempted to let the answering machine get it and finish her routine. But then she realized that it might be her father calling to tell her he was going to be late. *Or maybe he's checking up on me,* she added. *Making sure I'm right here where I'm supposed to be.*

"Ugh," she muttered, suddenly wistful for the days when she'd known her father trusted her. Hurrying over to the stereo, she turned off the music. Then she jogged out into the hall and grabbed the phone on the fourth ring, just before the machine clicked on. "Hello?" she said breathlessly.

"Hello, is Carole Hanson there, please?" an unfamiliar male voice asked politely.

"This is Carole."

"Oh! Hello, Carole. This is Craig Skippack— remember? From the Hometown Hope meeting today."

Carole's heart skipped a beat. Had they figured out that she wasn't really sick? she wondered, feeling panicky. Was this guy calling to kick her out of the group or something? Was he going to report her to Dr. Durbin?

"Hi," she said carefully. "Um, sure. I remember you."

"I hope you're feeling better," Craig said in a concerned voice. "Jan—er, Dr. Durbin—told me you had to leave early because you had a stomachache. I thought I should call and fill you in on what you missed."

"Oh, okay." Relief washed over Carole. "Um, I mean, thanks. I'm feeling a lot better now. But I appreciate your calling."

"No problem." Craig went on for a few more minutes, explaining the schedule for the upcoming park project. Carole scribbled down the dates and times and directions he gave her, along with his tips on how to dress and what to bring along.

When he was finished, Craig asked if she had any questions. She didn't, so they said their good-byes and hung up.

Wandering back into her bedroom, Carole glanced at the notes she'd made and sighed. It sounded like they would be pretty busy the following week. But she knew she would probably spend every minute wishing she were teaching lessons and cleaning tack and exercising horses at Pine Hollow rather than raking up trash or whatever else they were going to be doing at that park.

At least this Hometown Hope thing will get me out of the house, she thought, trying to look on the bright side—or at least the slightly less dark one—as she folded the schedule and tucked it into the frame of her dresser mirror where she wouldn't be able to misplace it. *And it will keep me away from Dad's disappointed looks.*

With any luck, it might even distract her from her own gloomy thoughts, her restlessness, her almost constant feelings of sadness, disappointment, and confusion. At least for a little while.

"Come on." Stevie finally managed to regain control of her limbs. She raced toward Blue, gesturing for Phil to follow. "Hurry! We've got to catch up to him before he hurts himself. Or Crystal."

"Right behind you," Phil said grimly, already heading toward Teddy.

Seconds later they were both in the saddle. As Stevie checked to make sure she'd tightened her girth enough, she flashed back and realized that A.J. hadn't done the same. Had he remembered to loosen it when they'd turned out the horses? She had no idea, and she was afraid to think about it too much. If his saddle slipped while he was galloping full tilt along the twisting, rocky trail . . .

"Be careful, Stevie," Phil shouted as they both urged their horses forward at a swift trot. "Don't take any chances with your own safety."

"Don't worry." Stevie clucked to Blue, who seemed a bit startled at their sudden departure. "Come on, girl. Mush!"

She led the way after A.J., whose yells were still drifting back faintly from the trail ahead. Behind her she could hear Phil talking to Teddy, urging him forward. Peering ahead through the trees, Stevie tried to judge how fast she could risk going on the trail. It was narrow, flanked on both sides by thick shrubbery, thorny berry bushes, and large boulders. But the ground directly underfoot seemed clear and solid enough. There hadn't been much rain lately, so the ground was dry and packed hard. Stevie could only hope that the trail didn't get rockier or otherwise more difficult somewhere past the twists and turns that hid it from view a little farther ahead.

When she was sure that Blue's footing was secure on the trail, Stevie nudged the mare into a canter. At that pace Blue had a long stride that ate up the ground beneath them. It was no gallop, but as Phil had pointed out, they couldn't take any chances. They couldn't help A.J. one bit if one their own horses broke a sesamoid bone or took a bad step and tossed its rider into the brambles along the trail.

At least A.J.'s got a chance of coming through this riding Crystal, she thought, trying to find any glimmer of good news in the situation. *She's a tough little mare, sound as can be. Those sturdy legs of hers can take a lot more abuse than most horses' legs can.*

Glancing down and forward, she caught a flash of Blue's forelegs as they pumped forward in a swift, rocking stride. She and Phil were lucky in their present mounts, too. Blue was a solidly built grade horse with heavy legs and thick bones. And as a quarter horse, Teddy was well suited to the trail's twists and turns. His agility, his solid knees and flexible hocks made him swift and surefooted on any terrain.

Stevie shuddered to think what she would do if she were riding Belle at the moment. Her mare was as sound and willing as they came, but she had the slender, finely boned, delicate legs that befitted her Arabian–Saddlebred heritage. Stevie couldn't imagine taking her over the trail so fast. Then again, she couldn't imagine just letting A.J. gallop off into the sunset, either.

"Come on, Blue," she muttered, leaning closer to the mare's neck and doing her best to concentrate on the here and now. "We've got to catch up to them. You hear me? I know you can do it, Blue girl. You're the greatest, Blue baby . . ."

She was so busy talking to the mare that she almost missed the sharp curve just ahead where the trail veered away from the river. The horse saw it, though, and she hardly slowed down as she spun around the forty-five-degree turn. Stevie gasped as she was thrown sideways by the sudden shift in direction. Grabbing a handful of Blue's mane, she pulled herself up again. Her right foot had slid partway out of the stirrup, but she jammed it back in place, wedging her heel against the metal tread before it could slip away entirely.

"Stevie!" Phil shouted from behind her. "Stevie! Are you okay?"

Stevie made sure she was back in control, getting a grip on the reins and checking her balance. Then she removed one hand from the reins just long enough to flash Phil an "A-OK" sign with her thumb and forefinger.

"Be careful!" he called, sounding worried.

"Back at you!" she shouted in reply, not sure he could hear her.

Then she returned her full attention to the trail, knowing that the next mistake could be much more serious. She strained her ears, trying to hear whether they were still on the right track. But A.J. had either tired of his cowboy whooping or had pulled too far ahead for her to hear him anymore. At least those were the only two possible explanations for his silence that she could stand to consider. . . .

But what if we're going the wrong way? she wondered anxiously. *A.J. isn't exactly following the rules here. What if he decided to crash off into the underbrush and make his own trail?*

A quick glance to either side convinced her that wasn't likely. If a horse and rider had plowed through the tangle of vines and brush along the trail, the destruction would be easy to spot. So as long as they didn't come upon any forks in the trail, they would just have to assume that he was somewhere ahead of them.

Stevie leaned forward again, trying to cut down on wind resistance to avoid tiring her mount faster than necessary. "Keep it up, Blue girl," she whispered to the horse. "All we have to do is keep going and we'll find him sooner or later. And everything will be fine." She crossed her fingers as she said it, praying it was true.

A few minutes later the trail emerged into a broad meadow. Stevie cantered out into it, then reluctantly pulled Blue to a trot and then a walk. The grass and wildflowers were dried and brown now from early-November frosts, but they still covered the ground like a carpet. There was no telling what kinds of rocks, tree branches, or animal burrows might lie beneath the thick growth.

Besides, this place might as well have a big sign saying Intersection, she thought ruefully, glancing around at the myriad trails leading out of the meadow in every direction. *How are we ever going to guess which way A.J. went?*

Phil caught up to her, bringing Teddy to a walk as well. "Give me a break," he said breathlessly, looking around. "So now what?"

Stevie shrugged and bit her lip, still looking around for some sign of which way A.J. had gone. "I don't know," she admitted. "Man, why couldn't you have joined the Boy Scouts instead of spending all your time in the saddle? Maybe then you could find some hoofprints or broken twigs or something and figure out which way he went."

Suddenly Phil grinned. "Hey," he said, pointing off to their left. "I may not be an Eagle Scout, but I think it's safe to say he went thataway."

Following his gaze, Stevie almost laughed out loud. Right there, visible even through the grass, was a fresh, steaming ball of manure. "Okay, you earned your merit badge," she said, turning Blue in that direction. "Check it out. It's practically pointing us straight at that wide trail up there."

"Let's go."

The two of them kept their horses together until they reached the edge of the woods. The trail in question was at least twenty feet wide, but Stevie dropped back, letting Phil ride on ahead. She had learned her lesson on the sharp curve. If they wanted to ride quickly, it would be safer if they didn't try to do it two abreast. The trail might narrow suddenly at any time.

She kept her gaze trained on Teddy's stocky, powerful hindquarters as Phil put him into a trot, then a controlled gallop. Blue hardly had to be told before she was keeping pace. Despite their wild ride over the first part of the trail, the mare barely seemed winded.

"That's my girl," Stevie said absently, patting the mare on the neck. But she was focused once again on worrying about A.J. and Crystal. A.J. might be bombed out of his mind at the moment, but she knew that when he came back to his senses he would never forgive himself if anything happened to his horse. She was sure of that. He might have changed a lot in the past couple of months, but he hadn't lost his old self completely.

The sight of Teddy stumbling just ahead jerked her out of her thoughts. "Phil!" she gasped, automatically pulling up on the reins. Blue tossed her head and danced to a halt, skittering to one side to avoid plowing into Teddy.

"Whoa, boy!" Phil cried. He had kept his seat, and he was able to guide his horse with his seat, legs, and hands. Teddy lurched back onto all four legs.

Glancing down quickly, Stevie saw the culprit—a large, loose stone that must have been partly buried in the dirt and fallen leaves. Then she returned her attention to Teddy as Phil slid out of the saddle and bent over his horse's right foreleg.

She bit her tongue, wanting to call out all kinds of questions but knowing that Phil would tell her what was happening as soon as he knew. "Feels okay," he called without looking up, running his hands over Teddy's leg from the knee to the hoof. But his face was still drawn and worried as he stepped to the horse's head and hooked his fingers through Teddy's bridle, tugging gently to start him walking forward.

Stevie hopped out of the saddle, leaving Blue ground-tied and praying that the mare was trained to obey. Then she hurried forward. "Here," she said, reaching for Teddy's bridle. "Let me. You look."

Phil nodded wordlessly and released his grip, stepping back with his gaze trained on his horse's legs. Stevie led Teddy forward. The gelding moved along agreeably without hesitation or resistance. *That's a good sign,* Stevie thought hopefully, glancing back at her boyfriend's face.

"So far, so good, I think," Phil said cautiously, echoing her thoughts. "Trot him, okay?"

Stevie broke into a jog, clucking to the horse. Teddy shifted into a slow, steady trot. Finally Phil was satisfied that the gelding hadn't hurt himself. "That was a close one," he said, giving Stevie a leg up into her saddle. Blue had wandered off the side of the trail to munch on some weeds, but she hadn't gone far. "Too close for comfort. We'd better not go so fast from now on, especially since we're heading back toward the river. It gets pretty rocky down there."

Stevie nodded. She could hear the faint sound of the tumbling river somewhere ahead and couldn't help feeling anxious. They had already lost time by stopping, and now they were going to lose even more. Glancing up at the tree canopy, she tried to judge how much daylight they had left. They hadn't brought flashlights or heavier jackets, so they would need to turn back soon. If they hadn't found A.J. by then, Mr. Baker and the police would have to rustle up a rescue party.

"Come on," she said, riding forward as Phil swung himself up onto Teddy's back. "Let's try a trot as long as it's still pretty smooth."

She clucked to Blue and they set off once again, this time with Phil and Teddy following behind them. For the next ten minutes the only sound Stevie heard from ahead was the rushing river, growing louder with every step they took.

But then she heard something else.

"Help!"

Stevie froze. "Did you hear that?" she called over her shoulder.

"I heard it." Phil's voice was grim.

"Help!" The voice came again, faint but unmistakable.

"That's A.J.," Stevie said, urging Blue forward a little faster. "He's in trouble."

Phil didn't reply, but Stevie could hear Teddy's hoofbeats coming faster, too. They rode in silence for another minute or two before suddenly emerging from the dim shelter of the trees onto a rocky plateau running down a hundred yards to a wide, boulder-studded section of the river.

Stevie stared in horror. A.J. and Crystal had plunged into the rushing, foam-flecked water.

TWELVE

Her heart in her throat, Stevie pulled Blue to a halt. "A.J.!" she shouted, trying not to sound as panicked as she felt. "A.J.! Are you all right?"

A.J. twisted around in his saddle and spotted them. "Stevie! Phil!" he cried. "Help! I—I can't—"

"Just hold on, buddy," Phil called over the roar of the current. He urged Teddy forward. "We're coming. Hold tight."

Stevie followed him across the rocky shore to the water's edge. There was a shallow, sedge-choked area where the muddy water hardly moved at all. But only a couple of feet out, she could see that the riverbed dropped off steeply. Crystal was floundering desperately against the current, trying to keep her footing in the rapidly rushing water, which splashed over her withers. A.J. had lost his hard hat sometime during his wild ride, but at the moment he was still keeping his seat in the slick, wet saddle. But just barely. He had dropped the reins and was clutching his horse's mane with both hands, his chest pressed against her neck and his knees gripping the saddle tightly. Water splashed his face every time Crystal moved, and his reddish brown hair was sticking to his forehead in soggy clumps.

"Don't let go!" Stevie shouted to him, pulling Blue to a halt at the water's edge.

Phil dismounted quickly and hurried up to the edge of the river. "See if you can get her turned around!" he called. "You've got to get her out of there."

A.J. nodded. Leaning back a little in the saddle, he reached down into the water, scrabbling for the reins. A moment later he came up with them in his hand, and he quickly tightened up on them and used them to guide Crystal's head back around toward the shoreline.

The mare lumbered awkwardly in a tight circle in the water, rolling her eyes and snorting in terror. "He's doing it," Stevie said tensely, sliding out of Blue's saddle while keeping her eyes glued to the waterlogged pair. Taking a step closer to Phil, she grabbed his hand for comfort. "He's aiming her back this way."

"Yeah," Phil agreed, squeezing her hand. "He is. Now if they can just—"

"Aaah!" A.J.'s terrified cry interrupted Phil's

words. For a second Stevie couldn't see what the problem was—as far as she could tell, Crystal was still making her way slowly against the current, toward the shore.

But then she saw A.J. drop the reins and grab wildly at the horse's mane again, and her whole body went cold as she guessed what had happened.

"The saddle," she gasped. "It's slipping, isn't it?"

Phil didn't bother to reply. He was already moving forward, still gripping Stevie's hand tightly, splashing into the shallows without seeming to notice the cold water swirling around his feet. "Grab her neck!" he shouted. "Just hold on!"

A.J. turned his head slightly, seeming to hear Phil. Unfortunately Crystal heard him, too, and shied away from his loud voice. She lost her footing on the rocky riverbed and nearly fell, thrashing wildly with all four legs. A second later she found her balance again, bracing herself against the jagged outcropping of a huge boulder that jutted out of the water just downstream. But her efforts had made the saddle slip even farther to the side, taking A.J. with it. He was still clinging to her mane, but Stevie could see that his hips were wedged between Crystal's body and the huge boulder.

"There's no way he can get up on her back," Stevie cried, her fingernails digging into Phil's palm. "Not in the condition he's in. If he slips down farther and she steps on him . . ."

She didn't dare finish the sentence, but it was enough for Phil. "Stay here," he said grimly, dropping her hand and shoving her gently away from the water. "I'm going in."

"No!" Stevie grabbed at his arm, but it was too late. Phil had already shrugged off his light nylon windbreaker and tossed aside his hard hat and was now wading determinedly through the shallows. A second later he took a big step down, the water surging from his ankles up to his waist. After a few more steps, he was all but swimming.

Stevie debated quickly about what to do. Her first impulse was to plunge into the river after him, but she knew that wouldn't do any good. It had been foolish for Phil to go in. The water was cold and the current could be deadly. It would only make things worse to have all three of them splashing around in there.

Phil was still inching toward his friend, forcing his way through the rushing current. The water was swirling around his chest, but he was wet to the top of his head because of the spray.

Stevie glanced out toward A.J. to see how he was holding up. Just as she looked their way, Crystal shifted her weight again and A.J.'s head slipped beneath the water. "A.J.!" Stevie screamed. "Phil, he's going under!"

Phil stopped trying to wade. He pushed himself forward, stroking strongly toward his friend. The current pulled at him, spinning him from side to side. But he kept swimming, fighting the swirling water with every kick. A.J.'s head popped above the surface and he gasped for breath before another surge swept over him and he disappeared again. At that moment Phil reached the boulder, grabbing at it just in time to stop himself from being swept right past.

Stevie bit her lip and watched Phil slowly, slowly pull himself around until he was close enough to duck under the water by Crystal's neck and grab A.J. He emerged with his friend's head in the crook of his elbow. A.J. sputtered and gurgled, but he seemed to be in one piece.

"Can you get him out of there?" Stevie yelled.

Phil didn't answer for a moment. He was too busy trying to yank A.J. out from behind his horse. Crystal wasn't helping much—every time Phil shoved at her, she leaned toward him stubbornly, still looking terrified. Finally Phil glanced at Stevie over his shoulder. "He's stuck!" he shouted back. "His foot. It slipped all the way through the stirrup. But that's not the worst of it—the reins got all tangled around his wrist somehow, and I don't think I can get them off.

Plus they're also caught in this big knot of water vines or something down below Crystal's chest, so even if we could get the bridle off I don't know how much it would help. We've got a real mess here."

Stevie felt panic overtaking her. She started to shake, and her mind refused to work right. What were they going to do? From what she could tell, it was taking all Phil's energy just to keep his own head and A.J.'s above the water. They couldn't move. They couldn't get themselves out of the freezing-cold river. And even if she rode for help as fast as she could, with no thought for her own safety, they were miles from civilization. She knew it would take too long—far too long—for her to return with help.

What are we going to do? she thought desperately, wincing as a wave crashed against the boulder and washed over Phil and A.J., hiding them momentarily. *What in the world are we going to do?*

"I had fun," Lisa said, smiling at Alex as she stepped up onto her front porch. "I'm glad your parents let you out."

"Me too." Alex reached for her, running his hands up her arms and then slipping them around her shoulders, pulling her toward him. "Really glad."

Lisa relaxed into his kiss. Almost. Part of her was still worrying over that funny feeling she'd had a few times over the course of their date. The feeling that something was a little off-kilter between them.

Finally Alex pulled away with a sigh. "I'd better go," he said softly, stroking her cheek gently with his fingers. "See you later, beautiful."

"Bye." Lisa smiled at him, then turned to let herself in through the front door as he loped off toward his own house. Her smile faded as she thought about that weird feeling. What could be wrong now, when Alex's grounding was fading, when it finally looked as though they might be back on track?

Maybe that's just it, Lisa thought as she went to the kitchen for a glass of water. *Maybe we're out of practice after all this time apart. It's only natural—we just need to get used to being together again. Sort of like how horses that have been out to pasture too long need to get used to being ridden again. They need a little refresher training, an attitude adjustment, just like us.*

Smiling at the image of herself and Alex as feisty half-wild horses, she nodded, satisfied that she'd hit on the answer. Soon, once Mr. and Mrs. Lake lifted Alex's grounding for good, they could all get back to normal. It would be about time.

The phone rang as Lisa opened the cabinet to get herself a glass. She started to hurry over to pick it up, then hesitated.

It's probably Dad calling to remind me to get some sleep on the plane so I'll be fresh for his week-long lecture about college, she speculated sourly. *Or maybe he just wants to get started on the lecture early, long-distance charges or no long-distance charges.*

She decided to play it safe and let the machine pick up. The phone rang twice more; then the recorded message clicked on. *"Hello, dear caller,"* her mother's voice trilled tinnily on the tape. *"You've reached the Atwood residence. Please leave a name and number so Lisa or I can call you back posthaste!"*

Grimacing as always at the supremely dorky message, Lisa waited for the beep as she set her glass on the counter. When it came, her mother's voice poured out of the tiny speaker again. "Hi, Lisa, it's Mom. I guess you're not home from your date yet. And guess what—" There was a girlish giggle. "Neither am I! Rafe and I are going to grab some dinner, then maybe catch a movie or something. I'll be late, so don't wait up!" After another giggle, the machine clicked off.

Lisa groaned and rolled her eyes, trying not to flash back to the picture of Rafe and her mother coming down to breakfast together the other morning. "Don't wait up," she muttered. "Yeah, right."

Suddenly talking to her father about college didn't sound like the worst fate in the world after all. It had to be better than hanging around home all week, worrying about what her mother and Rafe might be up to in the next room, feeling sad about Prancer, without even the comforting routine of school to distract her.

After all, I'm even feeling weird around Alex these days, she thought, filling her water glass and taking a quick gulp. *And that doesn't make any sense at all. So maybe it's really good that I'm going away for a while. Maybe I can clear my head while I'm out there. Get control of my feelings again.*

She nodded firmly, liking the thought of that—of getting away from her life in Willow Creek and figuring out how to feel normal again. Suddenly she couldn't wait to get to California, lectures or no lectures.

"Two and a half days and counting," she murmured. Setting her glass in the sink, she headed upstairs to start packing.

THIRTEEN

"This can't be happening," Stevie muttered anxiously, pacing back and forth on the shore and keeping her eyes trained on Phil and A.J. The situation hadn't changed much in the past few minutes. Crystal was still in the river, jerking around nervously. Phil was trying to keep A.J.'s head clear of the water without slipping down into it himself. And Stevie was racking her brain for a way to get them out of there.

Maybe I should just ride for help, she thought, casting a quick glance at Blue, who was standing quietly behind her with her head close to Teddy's. Both horses were munching on some dry grass they'd found growing among the rocks on the shore. Miraculously, they didn't seem to be catching Crystal's panic. *I could probably make it back to the stable in, oh . . .* Stevie calculated quickly in her head. Then she blew out a vehement sigh. *Oh, about an hour, if Blue suddenly turns into Secretariat,* she concluded grimly. *Too long. Way too long.*

Still, she couldn't just stand and watch. She had to do something, take some action—but what? There just didn't seem to be any good choices. Riding for help was out. Jumping into the river was out, too. She would have done it in a heartbeat if she'd thought she could help, but there was barely room for the two guys between Crystal and the boulder. Stevie wouldn't even be able to reach them unless she crawled right over the panicky horse.

"Damn!" she cried in frustration, pounding her hands on her thighs. "Ouch!" she added as her left pinky smacked into something hard and unyielding.

Stevie stuck her hand into her pocket to see what it was. She pulled out the folded Swiss Army knife.

"Oh, yeah," she muttered, remembering how she'd stuck it in there earlier after accidentally slicing A.J.'s shirt with it. She was about to return it to her pocket when an idea popped into her head. Holding the knife up on her palm, she stared at it for a moment. It belonged to her father, who took it on occasional fishing trips, and it was so sharp that he'd had doubts about letting Stevie take it that day. Now she was glad he hadn't managed to talk her into taking her brother Chad's old Scout knife instead.

It might work, she thought, weighing the knife in her hand and giving it a critical look. *And it might be our only chance. If only I can get close enough to try it without totally freaking Crystal out. Maybe if I can find something to use for a—*

"Aha!" she cried, spotting Phil's windbreaker lying on the rocky shoreline. Stevie leaped for it and immediately attacked it with the knife, hacking into the hem about a foot from the zipper and sawing upward. If they all came through this, she would personally save up her allowance to help Phil buy a new jacket.

She was concentrating so hard on what she was doing that it took her a moment to realize that her toes were now in the river, the water seeping through her leather riding boots. She stepped back from the edge, surprised at how cold the water was. It was November, and the sun didn't warm the river the way it did in the summer. The water stayed clear and frigid on its way down from the cold springs high in the mountains.

Taking a step back and casting a worried glance at Phil and A.J., Stevie returned to slicing through the thin nylon fabric, which turned out to be surprisingly resistant to her efforts. She sawed at it until it finally gave, ripping it in a clean, long slice.

Tossing away the rest of the jacket, Stevie slung the strip she'd ripped off around her neck, then hurried toward Blue. "Hey, girl," she said to the horse. "Feel like taking a dip?"

Blue blinked at her, hardly pausing in her grazing as Stevie quickly double-checked the girth and mounted. When Stevie picked up the reins and clucked to her, though, the mare obediently turned and headed out of the grassy area toward the rocky shoreline.

"That's right, girl," Stevie said soothingly as she guided the mare into the chilly, gurgling shallows. "Here we go."

Blue hesitated when the water swirled around her fetlocks. But as Stevie continued to urge her forward, the mare snorted and kept going. Soon she was splashing through the chest-deep water toward the others. Crystal saw her coming and rolled her eyes until the whites showed. But she didn't move, except to stretch her neck forward and snuffle at Blue's neck as Stevie guided her horse next to Crystal. Soon the two mares were standing nose to rump in an incongruous approximation of the way they might, in a very different situation, stand in the pasture flicking flies off each other's faces with their tails.

"You guys okay over there?" Stevie called,

leaning out of the saddle to peer over Crystal's broad back. Crystal didn't seem particularly happy about that—she tossed her head and then twisted her neck around awkwardly to try to see what Stevie was doing. But Stevie ignored the horse for the moment. She was more concerned about Phil and A.J., both of whom were turning an interesting shade of blue in the cold water. Stevie could see that Phil's arm, which was still clutching A.J.'s neck and upper chest to keep his head above water, was peppered with goose bumps. His other hand was clutching the edge of Crystal's tilted saddle to help keep himself afloat as waves of rapidly moving water swept past, lifting him off the river floor and bumping him against the boulder behind him.

"Oh, yeah," Phil called back breathlessly. "We're having a total blast. What are you doing in here? Shouldn't you be riding for the posse right about now?"

Stevie flipped open the knife and held it over Crystal's back so that he could see it. "I brought this. I think I can cut the reins with it and get A.J. loose."

"Well, what are you waiting for?"

Stevie stuck the knife between her teeth, feeling like a character in a bad action movie. But she needed both hands free for what she was going to do next. "You'll see," she told Phil, or at least that was what she tried to say. With the knife in her teeth it came out more like "Rrrr rrr," and Phil looked confused—and cold. Very cold.

Gripping Blue's saddle with her legs, Stevie leaned back and made a grab for Crystal's cheek piece. The mare saw what she was doing and tossed her head, moving herself out of reach.

Come on, come on, Stevie chanted in her head, leaning farther out of her saddle. *Just a little closer, that's it. . . .*

She grabbed again, and this time she felt cold, slimy, soaking-wet leather beneath her fingers. "It's okay, girl," she murmured around the knife, knowing that the horse wouldn't care if her words came out a little garbled. "I've got you. You're going to be okay."

Crystal snorted and pulled, almost yanking the bridle leather out of Stevie's fingers, which were already a little stiff from the cold. But Stevie held on. Still talking to the horse soothingly, she signaled for Blue to back up a few steps. The mare didn't respond at first, but when Stevie repeated the command more firmly, she reluctantly took a few awkward backward steps, giving Stevie easier access to Crystal's head.

Still keeping a firm hold on the bridle with one hand, Stevie dropped her own reins and grabbed the strip of nylon. "Okay, Crystal," she said soothingly. "There's a good girl."

Holding her breath, Stevie carefully placed the fabric over the horse's eyes, tucking it into the sides of the bridle to keep it in place. As soon as Stevie tightened the blindfold, Crystal calmed down a little. She was still snorting and shifting her weight, but at least she wasn't as likely to slip or bolt.

Okay, now comes the hard part, Stevie thought grimly. Rubbing Crystal's neck to comfort her and keep her aware of where she was, Stevie guided Blue forward a few steps until the mares' backs were lined up again, then she unbuckled the snaffle reins and pushed them forward, praying that the mare would still understand ground-tying even when the ground wasn't technically in sight. Giving her horse a pat, she kicked her feet free of the stirrups underwater.

"Hold tight, now, girls," she told the two horses. "Just stay still for me, okay?"

Stevie swung one leg over Blue's back, holding on to the pommel to keep from slipping off the wet leather seat. Soon she was perched in an awkward and precarious sidesaddle position. *Maybe I could just lean over and push the knife across the saddle to Phil,* she thought. But then she shuddered, imagining the knife sliding right past Phil's hand and disappearing into the chilly depths. Then they would really be in trouble.

She gazed at Crystal's back. The mare's saddle had slid about halfway to her left side, the side facing away from Stevie. It looked very far away. And there was no guarantee that it wouldn't slip back the other way if she grabbed it, dumping her right into the freezing-cold water swirling between two nervous horses. . . .

Stevie decided not to think anymore about how crazy it was to try what she was going to try. She just had to do it, that was all.

Taking a deep breath, she leaned over and grabbed for Crystal's saddle. Her fingers scrabbled for a hold as she lost her balance and slipped forward, her rear sliding off the sloped side of Blue's saddle as if it were a water slide at an amusement park. Just in time, she found the cantle with one hand and a hank of Crystal's wet mane with the other. She heaved herself ungracefully forward, pulling for all she was worth while pushing against Blue's side with her legs. She landed hard on her stomach on the edge of the saddle.

"Oof!" she gasped, almost spitting out the knife. She clamped her teeth together just in time, keeping it in place.

"Are you okay?" Phil was watching her anxiously. Even A.J. had turned his head to follow her progress.

Stevie couldn't answer. She was too busy trying to hold on as Crystal snorted sharply and did a sort of half buck in the deep water. Holding on for all she was worth, Stevie waited, praying that Blue wouldn't start to panic, too. If she did . . .

After a few endless seconds, Crystal quieted down again. Heaving a sigh of relief, Stevie inched forward until she was lying right across the middle of Crystal's back where she could balance herself. Only then did she release her grip with one hand and carefully remove the knife from her teeth.

"Okay," she said, aware that her teeth were starting to chatter. Her legs were now hanging in the river up to her thighs, her soggy jeans clinging to her skin. "Just show me where to cut."

"The reins are wrapped around his right arm," Phil reported. "A.J., can you move your arm closer? Stevie's going to try to get you loose."

A.J. nodded dully. There was a slight disturbance in the surface, and then A.J.'s arm appeared and Stevie could see the problem for herself. She gulped. She'd been pretty confident that she could saw through one layer of leather. But Crystal's long reins were wrapped around A.J.'s arm three or four times.

Still, it wasn't as though she had much choice. She had come this far. All she could do was try.

"Okay, hold still," she said as cheerily as she could. "Let's see if we can do this without drawing blood. Especially mine."

She pushed herself forward a little more, hooking one boot through Crystal's loosened girth to secure herself in position. She was going to need both hands for this.

Grabbing A.J.'s arm, Stevie pulled it a little closer. A quick glance at the crisscrossing leather straps gave her a pretty good idea where to start. Shoving a couple of fingers between the leather and A.J.'s skin, she slid the knife into the space she'd created and pressed upward, sawing back and forth as firmly as she could.

"Is it working?" Phil asked anxiously. Stevie's activity was mostly blocked from his view by A.J.'s head. "Is the knife cutting it?"

"I think so." Stevie clenched her teeth determinedly and sawed harder. The leather started to split and pull apart. "Yeah, it's coming! We're just lucky these reins are the plain leather variety instead of those fancy plaited ones."

"Yeah," Phil said with a short laugh. "We're rolling in luck today for sure."

Stevie could tell he was trying to stay upbeat, but she didn't have time to return his banter. She just kept sawing away, pulling the leather taut with her free fingers. It seemed to take forever before she was halfway through. But after that, things suddenly got easier. The leather gave out, stretching and then finally snapping in two.

"Yes!" Stevie cried. "That's one down."

She reached for the next strand, ignoring the protesting muscles in her neck, legs, and hands. Sawing away diligently, she managed to work her way through that piece of leather as well.

"How's it going?" Phil asked just as the rein came loose.

"Almost there," Stevie replied. "I think if I get this last bit off, we can slip his hand out through the other loop."

Her hand was starting to go numb, both from the cold and from gripping the knife so tightly. Knowing that she couldn't afford to stop and rest, she switched it over to her left hand. It was harder for her to handle that way, but she didn't have much choice.

"Okay, hold still, everyone," she said. Unfortunately Crystal didn't get the message. The mare shifted her weight just as Stevie tried to slide the knife under the last strand of rein. "Ouch!" Stevie cried as her hand jerked to the side and the knife jabbed into her right palm. Glancing down, she saw blood seeping out of the cut and swirling off in the water.

"What?" Phil cried. "Are you okay? What happened?"

"Nothing," Stevie said, clenching her jaw and willing herself through a surge of light-headedness. She could handle a little blood. "I'm fine. Just hang in there."

Returning her attention to her task, she carefully slid the knife into position. She had to saw more slowly with her left hand, but she kept at it with determination, ignoring the throbbing in her right hand as she gripped the leather. Slice by slice, the rein started to pull apart. Second by second, the cut she was making gaped wider and wider.

Just when Stevie was starting to think it would never happen, the leather snapped and floated off on the water's surface.

"Yes!" she cried again. "Okay, A.J., now pull your arm back toward you. . . . There, that's the way. . . ." Guiding his hand through the last few loops of leather, Stevie managed to get him completely free of the reins at last. "That should do it!" she called to Phil. She glanced over her shoulder at Blue, who, true to her quiet, unflappable nature, was still standing more or less where Stevie had left her, her muzzle just above Crystal's croup as she turned her head and pricked her ears anxiously toward all the human commotion. "Just hold still for another sec and let me get back on my own horse before you start moving around," Stevie went on, relieved that her mare hadn't wandered off. "These two have been amazingly good so far, but . . ."

She didn't bother to finish the sentence. Instead, she stuck the knife back into her teeth and concentrated on pushing herself backward off the saddle, wincing as her injured hand pressed against the unyielding leather. By wriggling her legs and body from side to side, she managed to ease herself down partway into the water. Then, twisting at the waist and hoping her luck would hold, she fished around in the water for Blue's right stirrup.

When she found it, she jammed her foot into it, then pushed off Crystal's back before she could chicken out. Pivoting on her right leg, she felt her ankle scream with protest. But she ignored it, lunging for the mare's neck.

She grabbed Blue's mane with both hands, still doing her best to ignore the searing pain in her palm. Feeling the knife slip in her teeth, she spit it out before she could slice her face open to match her hand. The knife flew forward and landed with a plop in the water just past Blue's right shoulder, sinking instantly out of sight. Stevie hardly noticed as she scrabbled to keep her balance in the stirrup. Miraculously, she managed to hold on and get her body twisted around and facing the right way.

Her left leg felt heavy and clumsy as she swung it over and searched out the other stirrup with her foot. "Good thing Max isn't here," she commented, mostly to herself. "I'm sure he'd yell at me for mounting from the wrong side." She giggled at her own dark humor. Then, realizing that her giggle sounded slightly hysterical, she gulped and did her best to get a grip. They weren't out of this yet.

"Okay, everybody ready?" she called once she was securely in the saddle with Blue's reins in her hands. "I'm going to unhook Crystal's reins so she won't have to pull free of that seaweed stuff. Then we'll take it from there."

"Go for it," Phil replied. "Meanwhile I'll see what I can do about this stirrup."

Stevie winced. She'd totally forgotten that A.J.'s foot had slipped through the stirrup. Still, she figured Phil could take care of that now that A.J.'s arms were free and he could help keep himself afloat.

Fortunately, Crystal's reins were attached to the bit ring with a simple buckle fastener. Even with her fingers clumsy from the cold, Stevie was able to detach the buckles quickly without dislodging Crystal's blindfold. Then Stevie turned Blue around and steered her a little closer to the other horse. Crystal was starting to toss her head nervously again, and Stevie was afraid they were running out of time. Maybe Blue's presence could keep her calm a little longer. . . . Soon Crystal's chest was bumping against Blue's girth. Crystal stretched her neck forward, sniffing curiously at the other horse.

"That's right," Stevie crooned, grabbing Crystal's bridle and tugging lightly to keep her close. "We're here now. All you have to do is follow us out of this nasty old river, okay, sweetheart?"

Crystal snorted and shifted her weight nervously. Stevie held her breath as she waited to see what the mare would do next. She was counting on the fact that horses were herd animals. They took comfort in numbers, a throwback to their wild days when the herd was the only defense against predators. Stevie let out her breath and smiled as Crystal snorted once more and then stood still, her head turned toward Blue's neck and her body braced against the current.

"Okay, now, girls," Stevie said, making her voice as soothing as possible. "What do you say we head back to shore now, okay?"

Before my legs freeze to this saddle, she added silently. Still, she knew she didn't have much to complain about compared to Phil and A.J. They had been in the icy current much longer than she had. She stood in her stirrups to give them a slightly nervous glance.

"How's it going over there?" she called to them.

"No luck so far," Phil answered shortly. "His foot is really jammed in there, and the laces on his boots are all swollen from being wet. And I can't get to the stirrup leather to unbuckle it—it's way under Crystal's belly, and I can't reach it without letting go of A.J." He sounded frustrated and, for almost the first time since Stevie had known him, on the verge of tears. "I can't get him free."

Stevie tried not to think about the knife. If she'd been able to hang on to it, they might have managed to cut A.J.'s boots off his feet or saw through the stirrup leather. But this was no time for might-have-beens. They had to figure out another solution. "If I can get Crystal to move toward shore, can you two just sort of float along?"

"Don't think so," Phil said grimly. "A.J. isn't doing too great. Besides, if we didn't have this rock giving us something to grab on to . . ."

Stevie nodded, chewing her lip anxiously. She saw the problem clearly now that Phil had pointed it out. At the moment the two guys were wedged against the boulder by the current as well as the horse's bulk. But if she dragged them out from its shelter while A.J.'s foot was still stuck, he would have no way to stop the river from pulling him under—especially if he was too weak and sluggish from the cold and the alcohol in his bloodstream to tread water.

Think! she chided herself, feeling panic start to creep into her mind. *There's got to be a way. We're so close. . . .*

Ideas flashed through her mind, each more elaborate and impossible than the last. Creating a sling out of their clothes and tying A.J. to Crystal's side. Luring Teddy into the water somehow so that Phil and A.J. could grab on to him to stay afloat. Diving under Crystal's belly to unbuckle her girth or the stirrup leather . . .

Glancing over Crystal's back again, Stevie saw that A.J.'s eyes were half closed. There was no more time for plans. Besides, sometimes the simplest ideas were the ones that worked.

She backed Blue up another few steps. "Okay," she called crisply, hoping she sounded as though she knew what she was doing. "Here's what we'll do. When I say the word, you shove A.J. toward me so that I can grab his hair. I'll hold him above the water, and you dive down and work on that stirrup buckle. Got it?"

Phil hesitated for a second. Then he spoke, his voice sounding a little firmer. "Okay. Say the word."

Now it was Stevie's turn to hesitate. Could they really do this? In A.J.'s condition he would probably hardly notice the pain of having his hair practically yanked out of his scalp, assuming that Stevie could hold on with her cold fingers and lacerated palm while simultaneously keeping control of two understandably nervous horses. Then there was Phil. After spending so much time in the cold, cold water, did he still have the energy to dive under and struggle with the buckle of the stirrup leather, which would be as swollen and slick as all the rest of the tack? And even if he could, would Crystal tolerate what he was doing down there beneath her vulnerable belly, or would she kick to protect herself? Stevie's head swam and she squeezed her eyes shut, trying to block out the image of Crystal's heavy, iron-shod hoof connecting with Phil's skull.

"Okay," she said, knowing there was no other way. She grabbed Blue's mane with her injured right hand, hardly noticing the new flash of pain. Then she shifted her weight, leaning out over the other horse until she could see the two guys in the water beyond. "On the count of three. One . . . two . . ."

At the end of the count, she leaned as far as she could over Crystal's back, stretching toward A.J.'s head as Phil gave him a forceful shove in her direction. A.J.'s hair was longer than he usually kept it—another sign of his recent rebellion that Stevie had hardly noticed until now. She was able to get her fist around a good-sized hank.

"Got him!" she cried.

Phil stared up at her, breathing hard. "Are you sure?"

She just nodded. Her leg muscles were protesting again from their unnaturally twisted positions. Another muscle, one just above her right hip that she hadn't even known was there, was twitching with pain as it stretched unbearably.

But she wasn't going to let go. She held firm, pulling A.J.'s head a little closer to Crystal's side. A.J. whimpered slightly but made no other protest.

Without another word, Phil pulled in a deep breath and plunged beneath the surface. The water was foamy, so Stevie had only a shadowy view of what was happening. She did her best simply to wait, to hold on, and to pray.

Phil stayed underwater for more than a minute, his legs kicking out behind him as he struggled with the stirrup. Stevie thought she saw A.J.'s booted foot, floating helplessly near Phil's head, kick him in the forehead once when Phil yanked at the strap. But she couldn't be sure.

Finally Phil surfaced, gasping for breath. "Whew," he choked. "It's really stuck in there."

"Do you want to switch places?" Stevie asked. "I could give it a try."

Phil shook his head firmly, sending droplets flying from his wet hair. "I'm already soaked and frozen," he declared, his words a little blurred around the edges. "Besides, it would be too complicated. Just give me a sec and I'll go back down."

Stevie knew he was right. Even though she ached to take a more active role, she simply checked her grip on A.J.'s hair and nodded.

Phil dived down a second time. This time he stayed under even longer, so long that Stevie's heart started to pound with worry. What would she do if he didn't come up? How would she be able to save him and still hold on to A.J.? How could she—

"Pheeeeew!" Phil's pent-up breath exploded from his lungs as he burst out of the water.

"Phil!" Stevie cried, so relieved that she forgot for a second what they were doing. "Are you okay?"

"A-okay," Phil replied, his breath ragged and quick. "I got it! He's free!"

FOURTEEN

Carole pushed her fork under a small mound of mashed potatoes. She scooped it up and stared at it, then lowered it to the plate again.

"Are you okay, Carole?" her father asked. "If the potatoes are getting cold, you could stick them in the microwave for a minute or two."

"No, they're fine." Carole picked up her fork and shoved it into her mouth, forcing herself to swallow. The last thing she wanted was to start her father off on a lecture about her moping.

"Um, so how did your speech go last night?"

"Just fine." Colonel Hanson reached for another slice of roasted chicken from the platter on the table between them. "It was just a small company I spoke to this time, so there were only about fifty people there. But a lot of them came up to me afterward to ask questions or say nice things about what I'd said."

"That's nice." Usually Carole loved hearing about the motivational speeches her father gave for corporations and other organizations. After his long, distinguished career as a Marine, he had a lot of interesting things to say to people about living up to their potential.

But today she wasn't in the mood. After all, wasn't he the one who was keeping her from living up to her potential by banning her from the one thing she was best at?

She banished that thought. Getting whiny and feeling sorry for herself wouldn't help the situation. Neither would snapping at her father. All she could do was find a way to live through it.

"So how was school today?" Colonel Hanson spoke up, breaking the silence between them. "Did you get that Spanish quiz back?"

"Uh-huh. I got a B." Carole knew that her father was paying even more attention to her schoolwork than usual lately. She couldn't blame him for that, really, but it still felt weird to have him checking up on her. She wasn't used to that. "And school was fine."

"Good, good." Suddenly Colonel Hanson glanced up from his plate. "Oh! I almost forgot. How was the volunteer meeting? When are you getting started on the first project?"

Carole swallowed hard. "Um, the meeting was fine," she said. "We're cleaning up a park over past Whitby Street. Starting Saturday."

She almost blurted out the rest of the truth—

that she'd left the meeting early to say good-bye to Samson. But she couldn't do it.

It's funny, she thought, *but there seem to be a lot of things I can't say to Dad these days. I used to think I could talk to him about anything. But with him so mad at me . . .*

Images flashed through her head. Samson standing at the bottom of that ramp earlier that day, posing as if to give her one last look before he left Pine Hollow forever. Starlight nuzzling Rachel, looking for treats, not knowing that she would be his new caretaker now that Carole couldn't look after him. Prancer lowering her head to the stall floor for the last time the other day, panting for breath even as the life left her big, dark eyes. The way Max had looked at Carole when she told him she had to quit— sympathetic, understanding, and yet disappointed. Ben leaning toward her, his eyes soft and questioning as his lips found hers . . .

It was all so difficult and confusing. And not having anyone to talk to about it made it even harder. She couldn't discuss it with her friends, since she wasn't allowed to make any phone calls and it was impossible to get a private moment with Lisa at school. It was bad enough being cut off from them. But it was even worse knowing she couldn't talk to her father.

She glanced at him again as she reached for her glass of water. *It's almost like he's suddenly changed,* she thought. *Become a stranger.*

But she almost immediately realized that wasn't quite it. It was more as if she were the one who had changed.

He's right when he says I brought this all on myself, she thought. *If I hadn't cheated on that test, I wouldn't be grounded now, and I'd still have my job. Max would still think I was a model employee and a totally honest person.* She grimaced. *I'd still think that about myself.*

She wished she could go back in time and fix everything. Knowing what she knew now, she would never have cheated on that test. She would have studied harder or just taken the F and made up for it somehow through extra-credit work. That would still have meant missing Pine Hollow for a little while, but it wouldn't have been as bad as this. Nothing would have been as bad as this.

Besides, she thought, *if I could go back, maybe I could catch Prancer's problems before they went so far. Maybe we could have saved her if we'd been paying closer attention, if we hadn't all been so busy getting ready for the horse show. . . .*

She wasn't sure whether that part was true or not, but thinking that there was even a slight chance that it was made her feel more miserable than ever.

And I would certainly know better than to hide what I was thinking about Starlight and Samson, she added, poking at her potatoes without seeing them. Instead, she was once again seeing Samson as she'd seen him earlier that day, stepping into the van with his head held high and proud. *This time I would talk to Max from the beginning. If he'd known how much Samson meant to me, maybe he would have helped me. We might have worked out some kind of deal—maybe he would even have taken Starlight as a partial trade or something to use as a school horse.*

That possibility hadn't occurred to her before. She sighed. It was just one more example of things she could have thought about sooner but hadn't.

And now it was too late. Short of a time machine, she had no idea what to do to make it all better. As she glanced at her father's face, so familiar and yet so distant now, she felt like running away and starting a whole new life somewhere else. If it hadn't meant leaving Starlight and her friends and the father she still loved—even if he didn't love her quite so much anymore . . . Well, it almost seemed worth it. After all, at that point it seemed as though her life might never go back to normal. How could it?

"May I please be excused?" Callie dabbed at her mouth with a napkin and glanced at her mother. At Mrs. Forester's nod, she pushed back her chair and picked up her crutches.

She was glad to escape to her bedroom and close the door behind her. All through dinner, she hadn't been able to stop brooding about everything that was bothering her. Her crutches. George liking her better with her crutches. Going back to Valley Vista with her crutches. Not being able to walk without her crutches . . .

"This is ridiculous," she muttered, clumping across the room toward her desk. Lowering herself into her chair, she held her crutches out in front of her and stared at them. They were just two pieces of metal with rubber tips on the ends and some padding across the tops. Why did they suddenly seem to have so much power over her?

It's all in my head, Callie thought. *That's the only thing holding me back. If I really believed I could walk without them, I could do it. My body's ready. It's my mind that doesn't get it. It's my mind that's too afraid to just go ahead and do it.*

That thought annoyed her. She didn't like being afraid.

"All right, then," she said aloud. "Let's do this."

She sat still in the chair a moment longer, visualizing what she was going to do. She was going to put her crutches aside. Then she was going to stand up and walk—all the way across the room to the bed. Without stopping. Without falling. Slowly and steadily.

Taking a deep breath, she turned and leaned her crutches against the edge of her desk. Then she pushed off the arms of her desk chair. When she was upright, she turned her head and looked at the bed.

The phone on her bedside table started ringing, but she ignored it. Someone else would pick up. She was totally focused, feeling the fierce, complete concentration she always felt at the start of a race. She was ready to go. Excited.

"Okay, let's do this," she muttered again. This time she stepped off with her weak leg. Her foot landed firmly on the floor. Her ankle wobbled slightly, but she just kept going. Left leg. Right leg again—

"Callie!" A loud, urgent knock accompanied her brother's voice. "Yo, Call. You in there?"

Startled by the sudden interruption, Callie swayed, grabbing the top of her dresser just in time to keep from falling. "What?" she yelled irritably. "What do you want?"

Scott burst in. His face was creased with worry. "That was Lisa calling just now," he said hurriedly, not even noticing Callie's consternation at his appearance. "Alex just called her—Stevie called him from the hospital. . . ."

FIFTEEN

"There's the turn up ahead," Lisa said, leaning forward to tap Scott on the shoulder.

"Thanks." He smiled and winked at her in the rearview mirror before hitting his turn signal. "But I've been to the hospital a few times myself lately, remember? I think I know the way."

Lisa blushed, glancing at Callie, who was in the front passenger seat. Of course the Forester family knew the way to the hospital. Scott's words were humorous, with no touch of irritation. But Lisa was aware that she'd been babbling worriedly during the entire ride. Ever since Alex had called her twenty minutes earlier, Lisa had been fretting over her friends' condition. According to her twin's report, Stevie swore that it had been a minor mishap and that everyone was going to be fine. But Lisa's pain over losing Prancer was too fresh and raw for her to believe it fully. She wouldn't be satisfied until she saw for herself that Stevie, Phil, and A.J. really were

alive and well. Lisa was glad that Scott had offered to drive them all to the hospital, since she
really wasn't sure she would have been capable of
concentrating on the road at the moment. And
Alex's parents had taken both of their cars to
their lawyers lecture a little while earlier, while
Stevie had driven her and Alex's car to Cross
County.

Reaching across the backseat of Scott's car for
Alex's hand, Lisa squeezed it tight. He glanced
over at her and smiled. "Don't worry," he said.
"We're almost there. Soon you'll be able to see
that they're just fine."

Lisa nodded. Alex knew her so well, and she
loved him for it. "I know," she said softly.

Callie twisted around in her seat. "So what do
you think happened?" she asked. "Did Stevie
give you any details, Alex? I mean, I didn't even
know they were out on the trails today. I didn't
see any sign of them at Pine Hollow."

"They weren't at Pine Hollow," Alex explained. "She went over to Cross County, and
they left from there."

Lisa nodded, remembering the many trail
rides she'd taken at Cross County Stables. "A lot
of the trails over there are rougher than the ones
we're used to," she told Callie and Scott. "Because of the river and the mountains. Around
Pine Hollow, most of the land is farmland or

sort of gently rolling forests with nice little streams running through them. Even the state parkland isn't too wild. But if you go a mile or so past Cross County's land into the part of the state forest that heads into the foothills, it can get pretty extreme."

"Hmm. Sounds like something I should check out once I start training again," Callie said thoughtfully. "It's always good to ride on different sorts of terrain."

Lisa shot her a quick, slightly surprised glance. She had almost forgotten that Callie had been a competitive endurance rider before her accident. *I guess her leg must be feeling stronger if she's thinking about training,* Lisa thought idly.

She didn't follow the train of thought any further, though. Scott had just pulled into the hospital parking lot. He found a space quickly, and all four of them hopped out of the car and moved toward the entrance.

"Shouldn't we be bringing flowers or something?" Scott commented.

Alex laughed. "For my sister? You've got to be kidding," he said. "And if I got flowers for Phil and A.J., they might get the wrong idea, know what I'm saying?"

It made Lisa feel a bit better to hear Alex joking around. After all, he was the one who'd actually spoken to Stevie. He couldn't be too worried if he was cracking jokes at her expense.

As they entered the hospital lobby, Callie nodded toward the gift shop on one side. "If we want flowers . . ." she began.

"I'll go grab some," Scott offered. "Although I can't claim to have the most refined taste in bouquets or anything."

Lisa smiled. "I'll help you," she said. She looked at Callie and Alex. "You guys find out what room they're in, okay?"

Alex nodded. "We're on it. See you by the elevator in a few."

Lisa felt a little impatient at the delay, but she thought it was a nice idea to bring flowers. Walking across the lobby with Scott, she scanned the display in the store window. "That one looks really nice," she said, pointing at a mixed bouquet of roses and hydrangeas. "What do you think?"

"I think you have excellent taste," Scott replied, giving Lisa an appreciative smile. "I also think it's a good thing you came along to help. I probably would have picked that one over there."

Lisa looked where he was pointing and laughed out loud. The bouquet in question was a bunch of bright pink plastic daisies with a tacky sign poking out of their midst, proclaiming IT'S A GIRL!

"Very nice," she joked. "Very tasteful."

"Hey, I know how to pick 'em," Scott retorted with a grin.

After paying for the flowers, the two of them hurried back to meet the others. A moment later Lisa spotted Alex and Callie coming toward them from the direction of the admissions desk. Alex was walking fast, but Lisa noticed that Callie had no trouble keeping up with him on her crutches. *She really does look a lot better,* Lisa thought. *She'll be walking without those things before we know it.*

"Second floor," Alex reported when he reached them. "Room two-oh-five. Phil and A.J. are roomies, and Stevie was never admitted—just treated and released."

Lisa was happy to hear that, though she still wanted to see for herself that Stevie was okay. "Why were the guys admitted?" she asked. "Do they have to stay here?"

"Just overnight, I think," Alex said, slipping his arm around her shoulders as Scott pressed the elevator button. "For observation or whatever. I guess we'll find out."

Soon they were on the second floor, where a friendly nurse pointed them toward the right room. The door was open, and voices drifted out into the hallway. "Hello! Anybody home?" Alex sang out.

Stevie jumped up from the visitors chair between the two beds. The room's privacy curtains were drawn all the way back, and Phil and A.J. were both sitting up against their crisp white hospital pillows. "Hi!" Stevie cried, hurrying around the end of A.J.'s bed. "Boy, you guys got here fast. None of the parents are even here yet."

"Including ours," Alex put in. "But Mom and Dad are probably on their way by now. I called and left a message for them at that lecture they went to." He grinned. "The way Dad was complaining this morning about how boring it was going to be, they're probably glad of the interruption."

Pushing him aside, Lisa stepped into the room to get a better look at Stevie. "So are you really all right?" she asked. Noticing a large bandage wrapped around most of Stevie's right hand, she pointed. "What's that?"

"Oh." Stevie held up her hand and grinned. "It's my excuse for not being able to take any tests at school for the rest of the week. I'm not allowed to write with this hand until the bandages come off. And when I try to write left-handed, it's just pathetic."

"Your regular handwriting's pathetic enough," Alex remarked.

"Hey!" Phil called, tugging at the collar of his pale green hospital gown. "Isn't anyone going to say hello to A.J. and me? We're the bedridden ones here, you know."

With that, everyone gathered around the two beds, asking a million questions at once. Meanwhile, Lisa pulled Stevie aside. "Did you call Carole?" she asked.

Stevie nodded. "I talked to the colonel," she said. "When I explained what happened, he let her come to the phone to say hi and hear the nutshell version of what's going on. But I don't think he would've let her out of the house to visit us for anything short of a coma."

Lisa shook her head sadly. "Poor Carole," she muttered. But there was no time at the moment to ponder Carole's crime and punishment. She turned her attention to Phil and A.J. "So are you two okay?" she asked, sizing them up. Both guys seemed a little paler and more subdued than usual, and A.J. had some nasty-looking bruises up and down one arm. Otherwise they seemed alive and healthy, aside from a few small cuts and scrapes on their faces. "I mean, what happened to you guys, anyway?"

"It's a long story," Phil said.

"Yeah," A.J. agreed. His voice sounded a little hoarse and scratchy. "And I don't come out very well in it."

Stevie shot him a look, then turned to the visitors. "We'll tell you everything," she promised. "But first the important details. I'm fine except for my hand. Phil has a few bumps and scrapes and is running a slight fever, so they're keeping him here overnight for observation in case it turns out to be pneumonia or something. And A.J. has more of those bumps and scrapes, along with a sprained ankle." She glanced over at him again. "Oh yeah, and a monster hangover."

Lisa's eyes widened. She shot A.J. a look, remembering the day the week before when she'd caught him drinking in a college bar. "Oh."

A.J. looked embarrassed. "Right," he said. "It's all part of the story. So why don't we get it over with?"

"If you insist," Phil agreed cheerfully. Scooting up a little farther in his bed, he cleared his throat. "It was a dark and stormy afternoon—"

"No it wasn't," Stevie interrupted, rolling her eyes. She returned to her seat between the guys' beds, waving Callie toward the second guest chair in the corner. Everyone else found perches on the edges of the beds or against the cabinets along the wall. "It was a gorgeous fall day. As most of you know, Phil and A.J. and I had decided to go for a nice, leisurely trail ride out at Cross County. . . ."

She went on to tell the whole story, with Phil

breaking in occasionally to make corrections or additions. A.J. didn't say much, though he paid close attention and nodded now and then.

After describing how Phil had finally freed A.J.'s leg from the stirrup, Stevie paused dramatically. "And that's when I knew we were all going to make it," she told her audience.

"Wow. But how did you get him out of there?" Alex asked. "I mean, even once his foot was free . . ."

"Oh, the rest was easy," Stevie said breezily, waving one hand in the air. "I pulled Crystal's blindfold off and gave her a slap on the rump, and she was out of the river like a flash. The only challenging part was holding Blue back so she wouldn't follow her—she was pretty sick of all that water by that point, too."

"Then what?" Lisa shuddered as she imagined trying to control a cold, wet, impatient horse in the middle of a rushing river, especially with a bleeding hand and numb, half-frozen legs.

"Stevie's being modest for a change." Phil spoke up from his bed. "Blue just about freaked out on her when Crystal went tearing out of the river. She was halfway after her before Stevie got her under control and turned around to come back for us." He shot Stevie an unabashedly admiring look. "And all while buckets of blood were gushing out of her hand where she'd cut it."

Lisa wrinkled her nose. "Eew," she said.

Stevie grinned, holding up her heavily bandaged hand. "Yeah," she said. "Wanna see?"

"No thank you," Scott answered for all of them. "So come on, don't keep us in suspense. What happened next?"

"Oh, right." Stevie sat back and glanced at Phil. "So anyway, good old Blue finally figured out that I was serious about going back in, and she turned right around and headed back to the big rock. I still had that blindfold, so I tossed one end of it to Phil. He grabbed it and got A.J. in a hammerlock with the other arm, and Blue and I dragged them right back to shore. Then we wrapped A.J. up in the rest of Phil's jacket, and I hopped on Teddy and went for help."

She didn't quite meet any of her friends' eyes as she finished, hoping they wouldn't press for more details about the last part. That ride through the darkening woods—trying to hurry without endangering herself or Teddy, worrying that she would get lost or not be able to direct help back to the guys, who were lying helpless, cold, and alone on the riverbank—had been a pretty intense experience. She really didn't feel like talking about it yet.

Callie glanced around. "Okay, since Carole's

211

not here, I'll be the one to ask," she said. "Are the horses okay?"

"I can answer that," Phil said. "I called Mr. Baker just before you got here to make sure he could get Teddy back to my place for me. He said Blue and Crystal are both going to be fine. They both had a few scratches from that wild ride through the woods—so did Teddy. And Crystal also had some huge, pointy stone stuck up in one shoe—he guessed that was why she didn't try to run out of the river sooner, and I'm guessing it may also explain why she didn't try to kick me while I was messing with that stirrup buckle." He shrugged. "She's got a pretty badly bruised sole from it, but he thinks it will heal just fine."

A.J. bit his lip. "Thank goodness," he said, so quietly that Lisa barely heard him.

Phil shot his friend a sympathetic glance. "Both mares were pretty well chilled, too," he told the others. "But they're tough. They aren't running a fever or showing any other lingering symptoms, so Mr. B. thinks they're going to be okay."

There was a moment of silence, everyone thinking. For her part, Lisa was trying simply to be thankful that everyone was okay, without imagining what might have happened if things had gone just a bit differently. If Phil hadn't been brave enough to plunge into the river after his friend. If Stevie hadn't stuck that knife in her pocket and it had been left behind with the other picnic things. If Crystal had broken a leg during that wild run. If Stevie hadn't been such a skilled rider, or if she'd been riding a more timid or skittish horse than steady old Blue. So many things could have changed the outcome of the day's adventure. . . .

A.J. was the first to speak. "Well," he said quietly. "You're probably all wondering if I've finally learned my lesson from this."

Lisa glanced at him quickly. She hadn't really thought about that yet, but now she did. All this had happened because of A.J.'s drinking. He'd put himself, his friends, and their horses in grave danger, all for a Thermos of vodka.

"Well?" Alex asked. "Did you?"

A.J. nodded. "For sure. This totally scared me straight." He grinned, but his smile faded almost before it began. "Actually, I guess I shouldn't kid around about this. I've been really stupid, and I just want to say I'm sorry. To all of you, but especially to Phil and Stevie." He looked over at the two of them, blinking rapidly several times. "I really owe you guys. Big-time."

For a second Stevie had the strongest urge to reach over and strangle him. Did he really think he could just apologize and everything would be okay? That words could make up for everything that had happened? How could he expect them all to forgive him for what he'd put them through?

Get a grip, girl, she told herself, digging her fingernails into her knees to keep herself from saying anything she might regret as the rage flooded through her, sharp and bitter. *Let it go. Just let it go. Everyone deserves a second chance— maybe a third and a fourth, even. Blowing up at him won't do any of us any good. It's all over now, and by some miracle, everybody's alive. That's all that matters.*

At that thought, the anger left as quickly as it had come. She leaned over and squeezed A.J.'s shoulder. "You don't owe us anything," she told him somberly. "That's what friends are for."

"Thanks." A.J. stared down at his bruised forearm for a moment before speaking again. "But anyway, you should all know that this is it for me. I'm not going to drink anymore. It's just not worth it."

"That's great," Lisa told him, more relieved than she could imagine to hear him say it. She just hoped he had the strength to stick to his vow. "It might be hard, though," she told him hesitantly. "Um, especially if, you know—"

"Lisa's being too tactful," Stevie broke in bluntly. "What she's trying to say is you've got to talk to your parents about this adoption thing. Or things aren't likely to get any better for you, drinking or not."

"I know." A.J. didn't quite meet anyone's eye. "I know. You're right. I'm going to—to talk to them. Soon."

"That won't be easy, either," Phil reminded him quietly.

A.J. rolled his eyes and chuckled weakly. "You're telling me," he said. "But I mean it. I'm going to do it—I have to. There's no way I can go on like this."

Lisa nodded, feeling proud of him. It had taken a long time, but A.J. had finally figured out that he was hurting himself with his behavior, as well as everyone who cared about him. Phil was right—it wouldn't be easy for A.J. to move on from here. Thanks to her parents' divorce, she knew as well as anyone how difficult it could be to pick up the pieces and face the future after everything you'd thought you could count on had changed. But Alex and her other friends had stood by her, and they would stand by A.J., too. Now that he was talking to them again, and as long as he *kept* talking to them, there would be plenty of support whenever he needed it. Lisa was sure that would give him the strength to go forward, just as it had done for her.

"Okay, I know I said no more drinking," A.J.

said, his voice hoarser than ever after his little speech. He grinned. "But I could really use a glass of water right about now. Phil's been hogging the pitcher over by his bed and I'm totally parched."

Lisa glanced over and saw the pitcher in question on a small table on the far side of Phil's bed. "I'll get it," she said, noting that she was the closest except for Callie.

Callie had just noticed the same thing. "No," she said quickly, not giving herself a chance to chicken out. "Let me get it."

"Are you sure?" Lisa looked at her doubtfully. "I mean, are you sure you can manage?"

In response, Callie pushed herself out of the chair, leaving her crutches leaning against the wall. *Okay, this is it,* she told herself. No looking back.

She focused on the water pitcher and took a step forward. Then another. And another. Left, right, left . . . Before she quite knew what was happening, her hand was reaching out for the handle. She hoisted the pitcher, being careful not to throw herself off balance, and turned, handing it to a gaping Phil so that he could pass it over to A.J.

"Callie!" Stevie exclaimed. "Check you out! You're walking!"

Callie grinned, realizing that it was true. She

faced her friends, who were all staring at her in shock and amazement. Callie was feeling pretty surprised herself. But more than that, she was feeling thrilled.

"Yeah," she said, keeping her voice casual. "Check me out."

But inside, she was singing for joy. She'd done it! She could walk again!

She glanced at Phil and A.J., who were still gazing at her with shock from their hospital beds. *I guess this is just one more happy ending for today,* she thought gleefully as she turned and walked back to her chair. Her steps were still shaky and slow, but that would improve quickly now that she knew she could do it. She grinned at her friends again as she sat down. *Yep,* she thought. *Definitely a happy ending!*

ABOUT THE AUTHOR

BONNIE BRYANT is the author of more than a hundred books about horses, including the Pine Hollow series, The Saddle Club series, Saddle Club Super Editions, and the Pony Tails series. She has also written novels and movie novelizations under her married name, B. B. Hiller.

Ms. Bryant began writing The Saddle Club in 1986. Although she had done some riding before that, she intensified her studies then and found herself learning right along with her characters Stevie, Carole, and Lisa. She claims that they are all much better riders than she is.

Ms. Bryant was born and raised in New York City. She still lives there, in Greenwich Village, with her two sons.